Neanderthal Wars

K Argyle

K P Whittaker

1

Best wishes

Keith

[signature]

No part of this book is to be copied or electrnically reproduced in any way without the prior permission of the Authors.

As Norak walked across to the pavilion building, he wasn't aware of being watched from the shadows. He knew there was rebellion in the wind, but didn't know from what direction it would come from.

Chapter One

Neanderthal Council:

The Neanderthal Council was gathered for their monthly meeting: Norak looked round at everyone and viewed them with concern, 'It has come to my attention that there are some of our people beginning to build up in rebellion against our Annarki Gods. There are those of our race that do not want to follow them, we need to stop this uprising very quickly before it destroys our society. If it's not stopped, it will create chaos amongst our race.'

Voix, the second councillor in command then added, 'It seems that these rebels do not like what we plan to do with the Annarki and want no connection with them. The Annarki are helping to strengthen our people and are going to build a new city where we can live amongst them and grow together. When this is achieved, we will be able to learn more from them and make our current society better.'

Norak then added, 'If anyone here hears anything about any rebels and who they are, please inform me or Voix immediately so we can apprehend them and keep them from getting stronger in their rebellion. They will be put in the compound where those who break our laws are kept until such time they are ready to conform to our societies ruling. If they don't reform and agree to our societies way of life after six months, they will be taken by the Annarki to the prison moon of Venbor, the most outer moon of the Annarki world. That is an ice planet where no one can live on the surface, but only live in the underground centre where they have hard labour tasks to do every day. There is no space craft based there so they cannot escape without freezing to death,' he said with great concern.

Everyone there who was sitting around the large oval table nodded their heads in agreement at what Norak had said.

Jarvoo looked around at the others observing their reaction to Norak's words, but he also had other issues to concern himself with at that time, and kept his silence.

<<<<< >>>>>

Jarvoo left the council building and walked towards another section of their town; he had very important news to pass on and knew it had to be delivered very quickly.

As Jarvoo left, Norak looked at Voix and said, 'I think Jarvoo has other things on his mind, he was up and left very quickly when we finished the meeting. That is unusual as he always has plenty to say after a meeting is finished, but he was off very quickly today, very strange, Norak said giving Voix a thoughtful look.

<<<<< >>>>>

Scaroon, the rebel leader was gathered with his followers, so far they numbered thirty-one; none of them wanted the Annarki as part of their lives, they wanted the old system retaining and were prepared to die if need be to stop the Annarki coming amongst them. Their first intentions were to put a stop to the joint building project of the new Annarki city on Thaldernian, their beloved planet.

Scaroon stood on a platform in an old building in the lower section of their town of Bordian. They secretly met in the old building that was no longer used by the townspeople.

'My friends and followers, I have received a message today from one of our spies, that the High Council is planning to catch us and put us into the criminal compound and keep us there until we agree with their plans of their jointly building a city with the Annarki. We all know that the Annarki just want to use us as paid slaves to build their city for them, and then they'll cast us out, but we are not going to let that happen, if we are able, we will stop the city being built in the first place, we will not be slaves to so-called Space Gods..'

Vertol, one of the rebels shouted out, 'Scaroon, what are we going to do first to stop the city being built? We know where they plan to build it.'

'We need to continue collecting explosives, so when they begin to build we can sabotage their work and blow it up when they have begun building, we need to slow them down as much as we can until we gather enough followers to start a revolutionary battle with them,' Scaroon told him.

'But, Scaroon, the Annarki have better weapons than us, our guns are primitive compared to theirs, many of us could die in an attempt to take over their people,' Morgot said.

Scaroon looked at him with an evil grin, 'In that case, we steal a ship and crew and also take their weapons. If we can steal a ship, we can attack them alongside the Greys as our allies. When we have stolen an Annarki ship, we will go to the Greys planet and tell them our plan. We can then use weapons from them too. The Greys have been at war with the Annarki for many years and each is trying to destroy each other's planet. We need the Greys on our side to win.'

Garma, another rebel said, 'Scaroon, you are aware that the Greys want our planet to rape it of its resources don't you, they may double-cross us, they can't be trusted.'

Scaroon looked at Garma with an unfriendly look, 'Garma, if we can get the Greys on our side they will be very grateful for the information we have. They will then make us part of their peoples forces, we shall all benefit from the mining of our planet and get rid of the Annarki who I trust less than the Greys.'

Garma nodded and said no more realising he had stirred Scaroon's anger at him. Scaroon was known to be somewhat short tempered and trigger happy, so he backed off and said no more.

<<<<< >>>>>

Norak and Voix were sitting in Norak's living quarters where Norak and his family relaxed in the evenings. Voix was feeling concerned about the rebels, 'Norak, I feel that the rebels are gaining more supporters and could become very dangerous. They are very secretive and we have no way of knowing how far they will go to stop us working with the Annarki. We don't even know where they meet in secret, and at this time they have the advantage.'

'I know this, Voix, we need to find out more about them and get to know what they are up to. I have considered trying to get someone to infiltrate them and become a spy, that way we will know what their intensions are,' Norak told him.

'That plan is good, but who is prepared to be a spy? Their leader, whoever he is, wouldn't hesitate to kill any spy within his rebels. Whoever wanted to become a spy would have to go with others who want to join them and make it look like he is going to follow their plans,' Voix said.

'We would have to select a man or woman who would fit in with them, he or she would need to be able to move fast, and be very careful and not to get detected, or they would be in great danger. We don't know who their top leader is yet, and that is the most important fact we need to know. We can then find him and bring him to justice and make an example of him, the chances are it is a man, but I wouldn't put the possibility of it being a woman out of the equation, only I will know who the spy will be, that way there is no way anyone will know,' Norak said.

'That is a good plan, but can't you tell me, Norak?' Voix asked.

'No, Voix,' he said wondering what the possibility would be of it being a woman, 'if only I know, it means no one can be accused of betrayal only me, and I can assure you, it isn't me. I will begin trying to find a faithful spy who would be prepared to help us and offer them a good reward for their bravery and devotion to our Neanderthal society,' Norak assured Voix.

'I understand,' Viox said and then got up and left Norak to his thoughts, 'I'll speak with you later Norak,' he said as he walked out of the conference room.

<<<<< >>>>>

After Voix left, Norak began to think who would be a loyal spy and be completely trustworthy. Several options passed through his mind then suddenly he had a wave of inspiration,

"Roella," his most trusted house keeper who had worked for him for several years, he knew she was able to take care of herself and was an unharmed combat instructor in her private life. She was also Shalaine's best friend, Shalaine being Norak's daughter.

Norak sent for Roella to ask her to come and see him, he thought he had the perfect spy. The following morning, Roella came into Norack's private room where he conducted his daily business.

'Good morning, Norak, I got the message from Shalaine that you wished to speak with me, what can I do for you?' she asked curious as to his reason for wanting to see her.

'Come in, Roella and have a seat, I have an important task for you if you are prepared to take it on.'

Roella was curious and looked at Norak with a questioning look, 'I'm intrigued, Norak, what is this task you speak of and why have you decided I would be the best one for it?' she asked.

Norak looked at her intently and began to speak to her in a very serious tone, 'Roella, you are aware that there is a group of rebels trying to disrupt the people and are trying to stop the Annaki from helping us build the new city we have planned.'

'Yes, Norak, but I have not given it any serious thought and took it that you have it all in hand to stop them.'

'Yes, that is true, but we don't know who their top leader is, whoever it might be, he or she is being very secretive and keeping very low and out of view to everyone else. What we need is a spy to infiltrate them and let us know who it is. I wondered with your fighting skills and fitness that you might be interested in the job, you will of course be well paid for it.'

Roella smiled at Norak and felt flattered that he had considered her for the task. She had a better idea. 'Norak, I am flattered that you consider me good enough, but I have a better idea to put to you. I am very well known in our city as I run classes for my fighting skills in different parts on different days, even your daughter Shalaine has now joined us and learning the skills I teach. Has she not told you about the lessons?' she asked.

Norak grinned at her, 'No, she hasn't but what is your alternative idea? I'm eager to know what it is?'

'Well, Norak, my sister, Kaleena is very skilled too, but doesn't live in our city; she lives a few miles away in Terone, a small town south of here. She would be perfect for the job and no one knows her in this city, if she went as your spy, she could relay the information you want to me and I could pass it on to you. How does that sound?'

Norak pondered for a few moments and then gave Roella a wide grin, 'Yes, Roella, that would be a good idea, but I would need to speak with her away from the council building and my home.'

'That isn't a problem, Norak, you could get disguised as I could and we could ride out and see her, that way, no one will notice us leaving and think we are just two riders going through the city, which happens all the time.'

'Very good, Roella, we can go tomorrow, will that be alright with you?'

'Yes, I will meet you outside the Education Building at mid-day, will that be suitable to you?' he asked her.

'Yes, Norak, I will see you then, but get yourself well disguised,' she said.

'Worry not, Roella, even you won't recognise me.'

Roella laughed at him gently, 'Perfect, I will be riding a black horse with a white muff around its nose, if I don't tell you that, you wouldn't recognise me either,' she said with a grin.

'Very well, I will meet you tomorrow as we have arranged.'

Roella left Norak and went to prepare herself and decide what she was going to wear as her disguise.

<<<<< >>>>>

Norak rode up towards Roella and saw her horse with the white nose muff on it. Norak was disguised very well, he looked like an old man with a long white beard and moustache and grey tattered hat and an old dark brown cape. He was normally clean shaven and dressed very smartly for the times. He noticed that Roella was wearing a wig showing a darker colour hair and she had darkened her skin tone to make herself look older.

'Hello, Roella, you are very convincing and have a good disguise, if you hadn't have told me about the white nose muff on your horse, I wouldn't have recognised you.'

'You look good to, Norak, I wouldn't have known it was you either if you hadn't have spoken to me.'

They began to ride out of the city towards the southern end and towards the town of Terone where Kaleena lived.

It took them about an hour to reach Terone and to find Kaleena's house. There were many people around going about their daily activities and no one questioned them being there. The disguises were working well.

They dismounted and tied theie horses up outside Kaleena's house on a small fence that surrounded her front garden area. This was a distinctive part of the houses in the town; each had a small front garden with a larger one at the rear.

As they went into Kaleena's house, she greeted them and Norack was surprised to see a beautiful young woman who would turn any man's eyes. She wore a slim fitting dress and sported a low cleavage front. Her dress was in an emerald green of a smooth satin material.

Kaleena saw Roella and smiled at her sister with the disguise she was wearing and gave her a sisterly hug. 'Roella, why are you dressed like that, and who is the old man with you?' she asked her looking back at Norak.

Norak spoke before Roella could answer, 'Kaleena, I am really a young man and this is my disguise, we will explain to you why, but may we sit somewhere first, it may take a little time to explain things. I am in reality, Norak, the head councillor in our town where we live in Bordian.

Kaleena looked at them both, 'I'm now very curious, when my sister comes to visit and disguised, there has to be some strange reason for it. Please sit over by the fire and explain, you have sparked off my interest and curiosity.'

Roella looked at Kaleena seriously, 'We are here on a secret mission, and Norak wants you to be a key part in it if you wish to take on the task, but we will understand if you don't wish to. It could involve great danger.'

Kaleena looked at Roella and then to Norak, she asked, looking at him, 'So what is this dangerous task you speak of?'

Norak began to tell her, 'Kaleena, you possibly know that the Sky Gods, the Annarki want us to help them build a city and share their knowledge with us. Well there is a group of rebels building up and are planning to stop the Annarki and will try to take over our council and rule with their increasing numbers. Our problem is, we don't know who their leader is or where they meet. We want someone who is able to look after themselves to join the rebels as a spy and eventually relay the information we need back to us, at the high council, so we can stop them. We hoped you might be interested in the task, Roella tells me that you too are very good at unharmed combat.'

Kaleena looked at Norak with a blank expression, and then gave a slight nod, 'I am prepared to do this for you, Norak. But I will have to do it on my terms and time, I will find my own way to get into the rebels numbers so it looks like I am a natural rebel and believe in their cause. It could take some time. I will need a place to live in your city and a job of work. It's no good teaching with Roella as they will suspect me very quickly; I need a job or business to give me a solid story so I can get to know the right people and get to the rebels without casting suspicion on myself.'

'I agree, with you, Kaleena and I have money with me to give you, it will be enough to set yourself up in some kind of shop, ordinary jobs are hard to come by, but I can help you find a place to set up a business, but no one will know that, only us three.'

Kaleena suddenly gave Norak a strange look followed by a wide grin, 'Norak, what would the rebels need to help them takeover?'

'I'm not sure what you mean, Kaleena, they certainly need more followers,' Norak said with a questioning look knowing that he felt it wasn't that, that Kaleena was suggesting or asking, 'What are you asking me, Kaleena?'

'Well, Norak, they are going to need any kind of weapons they can get their hands on, so my business could be a weapon supplier and have a range of guns and other weapons that people could buy, it could be popular with those who are not with the rebels too.'

Roella butted in, 'That would certainly attract the rebels to you, Kaleena, but isn't it making things more risky for the council to apprehend them if they have such weapons?'

Norak looked at Roella and added, 'That's a good point, Roella, but they are going to get them from elsewhere if Kaleena doesn't have a weapons shop and if she can supply them, there is a better chance that we can find out who their leader is and where he is operating from, and give Kaleena an easy access to joining the rebels.'

'That is true, Norak, in that case, the gun suppliers is a good idea, but how soon can it be set up?' Roella asked.

'I will let you know when I have found a business premises for you, Kaleena and tell Roella to let you know. The money will set you up. We will be in touch with you again soon; we have to go now before anyone starts to ask where I've been.'

'Very well, Norak, I will wait until I hear from you and put this money is a safe place. If the shop premises are large enough, I will be able to use the upstairs part to live in.'

'Yes, Kaleena, that is what I hope for too, I will be in touch through Roella, meanwhile, keep a low profile and don't attract any attention to yourself.'

'That's fine by me, I will look forward to setting the shop up and I hope it won't be long before the rebels get in touch with me.'

Chapter two

Greylon Defection:

Ashtuck, the captain of the leading patrol ship Cronod, looked at the front projection screen and observed a tiny spot on the horizon of the fourth planet Thaldernian. He turned to his first officer, Zigg and said, 'What have you on the distance viewing screen, I can see something on the front viewer in the distance that looks like it's approaching us, it looks from where I can see like a Greylon ship, but it's alone.'

Zigg immediately put the oncoming ship on the distance viewing screen and expanded the view, 'It's a Greylon ship, Captain, and you are right, it is alone, which is very unusual, shall I target it with our lasers?' he asked.

'No! Let him get closer and I'll contact it and see who is aboard and why it's alone. Greylon ships usually move in shoals of at least ten ships, something is not right with this one, I want to know what their mission is before destroying it.'

'Very well, Captain, I will keep the weapons on standby in case it opens fire on us, the shields are in operation.'

As the Greylon ship approached, Ashtuk and Zigg watched it as it came closer at a mid speed. Ashtuck voiced into the forward communicator, 'Greylon ship, identify yourself or be destroyed,' he said in a calm but firm voice.

Moments later, the leader of the Greylon ship came on screen on the large monitor above the forward viewer,

'Please do not fire on us, we are not intending any aggression towards you, we are rebel Greylon's and wish to join with the Annarki.'

Ashtuck looked at the Greylon facing him on the screen, 'Who are you?'

The Greylon looked at him as though he was in the grip of a vice about his face. 'I am Shnark. I have ten more with me, we wish to join with you, we have secret weapons technology, and are willing to trade it for a safe meeting with your leader, Barook,' he said in a very nervous voice expecting their ship to be blasted at any moment.

'How do we know that it's not a trick to destroy our planet with your secret weapon?' Ashtuck asked.

Shnark lifted a display device that had a diagram of a secret weapon shown on it. Ashtuck looked at it and at the same time, Zigg scanned it and transferred it to their techno-screen so their computers could examine it for any unseen explosive devices. Zigg looked at the Captain and said, 'It seems genuine, Captain, there are no explosive devices, only a diagram of how it would work.'

Captain Ashtuk looked back at Shnark, 'Why would you want to betray your own people, this has never been know before?'

Shnark looked at Ashtuck very nervously again, 'Because we don't agree with the aggression shown your people and wish to be part of your race and help the Thaldernian's live in peace and help you with them in any way we can.'

Ashtuk was still not convinced at Shnark's words, 'You may come to our ship and dock onto it, but only you will be allowed to board ours, we will also require to put a security team on your ship to guard the other ten Greylons, do you understand this request, if you don't agree, we will destroy your ship.'

'We will agree to your request, Captain. We will approach your ship and dock onto it.'

Shnark and the ship he was on, slowly moved close to the Annarki ship and docked onto it. Twelve Annarki security guards went onto the Greylon ship with hand weapons and surrounded them whilst they sat on a group of seats in the centre of the Greylon Control room. Shnark was taken aboard the Annarki ship with two other security guards to meet with Ashtuk.

He was taken to the bridge and had brought with him the viewing device he'd shown Ashtuk on the screen. He sat down facing the Annarki ship's Captain and was asked, 'What is this new weapon you wish to share with us?'

Shnark began to explain how this new weapon worked, 'The weapon is called "The Whisperer" we call it that because when it's fired it doesn't give off a detectable trail and is unable to be seen on any other ships scanners. We also have a scientist with us who deals with Greylon advanced weaponry, who has his own design that could be built to detect the whisperer if it is fired by the Greylons. This would give you an advantage so you can destroy the missiles when fired at the Annarki before they can destroy your ships.

Ashtuk listened to him with intrigue, he still wasn't convinced that Shnark was offering him something that would justify taking him to meet Barook. His next question was, 'How do we know that this will work and not just a story to sabotage our ships and things on our planet. You have to admit, Shnark, it sounds a bit like a clever plot by the Greylon's to defeat us and we will not be beaten and never will be by another inferior warring race.'

Shnark was understanding and knew that he had to find a way to convince Ashtuk he was telling the truth. Suddenly he had an idea that Ashtuk might listen too. 'Ashtuk, one of my men is called Jarako. He is the scientist I told you about who knows about the new weapon technology and helped to develop it, he also has an idea that could make your craft go faster and travel at unbelievable speeds, you would be able to travel to the stars and maybe even other galaxies, it's what's known as a *"Tachyon drive"*.'

Suddenly Ashtuk's ears pricked up, 'Does Jarako have his designs with him?'

Shnark realised that Ashtuk was suddenly listening to him, 'His designs are in his head and haven't been put down on any design surface, but he could explain how it worked in principle if you asked him.'

Ashtuk looked at one of the security guards with Shnark, 'Go and bring Jarako to me from the Greylon ship.'

The security guard went immediately to fetch him. It didn't take long before the guard came back with Jarako. Ashtuk looked him up and down and asked, 'What is this Tachyon drive that Shnark tells me about?'

Jarako looked at Shnark and then back to Ashtuk, 'It is the most advanced technology in the galaxy and it's my own design, the Greylons don't know about it and I have only recently designed it and is the most advanced propulsion system ever conceived.'

'So how does it work?' Ashtuk asked.

'Jarako said, 'Well it's so advanced it would be difficult to explain, but the universe has Tachyons flying through it all the time in innumerable amounts. To use it for a propulsion device, one would have to build a device that can capture them and convert them into a containment vessel so they can be controlled and converted into a propulsion drive.

They travel at the speed of light at their slowest speed, but could be made to travel at several times faster. Nothing would be able to catch a craft with such a propulsion drive.'

Ashtuk asked, 'And you know how to build a device that can work?'

'Yes, it's all about building the right magnetic device to attract the tachyons and then redirect them and process them to give you the propulsion drive.'

Shnark looked at Ashtuk and asked, 'Do you now believe what we are saying and what we want to do?'

Ashtuk looked at Shnark with a deep look and was still unsure about believing these two rebel Greylons, 'I still find it hard to believe that you have such technology and want to share it with us. I will contact Barook and tell him of this sudden betrayal of yours to join our people; he will want to be sure you are genuine in your actions before allowing you to come to our planet. He will wish to speak to you through our communications first.'

'We understand that, Ashtuk, we will wait until he wishes to speak to us.'

'Very well, you two will be taken to secure quarters and your other men will be kept separated in other quarters, just for security reasons. But I warn you here and now, any show of a threat to our people on this ship and you will all be vaporised on the spot, do you understand?' he asked Shnark in a very stern voice.

The Annarki security took them and placed them into secure quarters, and the same for their fellow rebels who were still on their ship under guard. When Ashtuk was satisfied, they had been placed safely in secure quarters he contacted Barook.

Barook appeared on the large communications monitor at the front of the Bridge's forward bulkhead. 'Hello, Ashtuk, what is so important that you have to contact me from your ship?' he asked in a stern sounding voice, even though Ashtuk was a long-standing faithful patrol ship Captain.

'Greetings, Barook, we have some interesting news for you, we have a group of Greylon rebels on our ship who wish to join us and claim to have designs for an advanced weapon called, "The Whisperer" that the Greylons have developed on their planet. However, one of the group is an advanced weapons scientist who has designs for a weapon that can detect the Whisperer weapon when it's fired on our ships and would allow us to detect the missiles and destroy them before they reached us. The scientist also claims that he has a new advanced propulsion system that can make our ships travel at several times the speed of light.'

Barook looked at Ashtuk with an expression of thunder about to burst on humanity, 'What! You've got What? Greylons on your ship! Are you out of your

20

thurking Annarki mind? I don't care what they have got, I don't care if it's a dammed creation machine, we do not allow Greylon's on our ships. These weapons had better be what they say they are or they shall be destroyed in a very painful way, and you will be demoted to a ships hold worker,' he howled at Ashtuk.

Ashtuk almost shrivelled into space dust, 'But, Barook, if what they have is genuinely true, we would have the perfect weapons to destroy the Greylons, once and for all and take over their planet, or maybe destroy it if need be. Let alone their new propulsion technology.'

'Ashtuk, don't *but* me, bring them to your bridge and I will see them and speak to them myself, they had better be right and can prove what they say or I will have them vaporised and you don't really want to know what I'll do to you. One more thing, I want this done, Now!' and I mean now! If not sooner!'

Ashtuk looked with sheer horror and ordered his security officer and said, 'Fetch Shnark and his science friend here now!'

The security officer literally ran from the bridge and fetched Shnark and Jarako so quickly, it was almost as if they had been teleported to the bridge. They stood before the screen where Barook was watching them arrive.

Barook looked at them with searing eyes, 'I am Barook, the overall leader of the Annarki, I warn you now, Greylons, you had better be telling the truth or you'll be vaporised on the spot. Now explain these weapons and advanced drive to me, and be careful, one slip and your gone, do you understand!'

Shnark looked at Barook on the screen with his whole body almost shaking, 'Lord, Barook, we come to you with advanced weapons and a new incredible propulsion device.'

'Well, firstly, why have you suddenly decided to want to join our people, this has never been known before, we have never trusted your race and never will, our ultimate intension is to destroy you from the galaxy, as soon as possible!'

'We can understand that, Barook, but our intentions are genuine, we really have what we say we have.'

'So you can understand me, hey! You must be a very clever man, not even my mistress can understand me, so how is it you think you can, get this clear, Greylon, we hate your race with vengeance and intend to destroy it.'

'Please accept what we say, Barook, we hate what our people are doing, we want to help the Neanderthals on Thaldernian, we don't agree with what our people want to do. Please accept what I say and allow us to come and show you our plans and designs.'

Barook looked at him as though dissecting every molecule of his body, 'Very well, Greylon, you may come to our planet with Ashtuk on his ship, I will come aboard and you and your scientist can show me what you have, but it had better be worth my time, or your days will be ended.'

'I promise, Barook, it will be worth your while, we will prepare our designs to show you in detail, we promise you that you will like what you see.'

'That is a wild promise. You obviously don't know me very well. I expect pure perfection in everything, that is how we have survived for so many eons. Now go to work and pray you make me satisfied, but, be warned, it had better be better than good. I will expect what you have to show me to be put into action immediately on completion. If I agree with it, it had better be convincing or you and your measly rebels with be no more,' Barook said in a slightly quieter voice, but in such a tone as to say, don't let me down.

The viewing screen went off and Shnark and Jarako were standing there as though they had been struck by lightning. Ashtuk looked at them and said, 'I advise you now, do not let Barook down or your lives will end very painfully, together with your friends. My guard will take you to our laboratory where you can draw out your plans in detail and make them clear to follow. Barook as you heard, does not take second best, they must be perfectly designed and pray they work when built.'

'I assure you, Ashtuk that they will.' Shnark said as they both nodded to him.

The security officer took them to the ships laboratory and they began their work immediately.

Chapter three

Arms for sale:

Norak was reading in his library when his mistress, Romanta came in, 'Norak, you have a visitor, it's Voix, is it alright to show him in?'

'Well, Romanta, I was just enjoying a quite time with one of my reader plaques, is it urgent right now?'

'It seemed to be, Norak, he looks a bit agitated about something.'

'Very well, show him in, I'll see him, he is my second councillor after all,' he said in a non-plus tone.

Romanta showed Voix in and he sat in the chair opposite Norak, 'I'm sorry to disturb you, Norak, but I have news of the rebels, I have heard they are growing in numbers quicker than we thought, they have nearly fifty now and rumour has it that more could be joining them.'

Norak looked at Voix with a serious look, 'We need to find out who their leader is, until we catch him or her, we are almost powerless. Whoever he or she is, is keeping themselves out of the picture.'

Voix looked at Norak very worried, 'Have you found a spy for us yet?'

'Only I will know that when it happens, but I'm not sure about the idea, I don't like putting someone in danger, I would feel very bad if someone we used was murdered for our benefit.'

Voix was surprised at what Norak said, 'But if we don't have a spy to find out who their leader is, how are we going to find their top leader.'

Norak looked at Voix with a questioning look, 'That would suggest that there is more than one leader organising the rebels, if that is the case, then they are planning on gathering more than we think, but I still feel unsure about putting someone in undercover as a spy,' Norak said.

Voix wasn't sure how to comment to Norak's words, 'I think we are going to have to be very careful, Norak, things would suggest that they have got an ultimate plan and it's not far away. Have you any idea what it might be?'

'No, Voix, but I am increasing our armies recruiting too, I think there could be an uprising on the way and I want to be ready for it.'

Voix nodded, 'That might be true.' Voix looked at Norak and said, 'I have to go, Norak, I am meeting my mistress to take her to buy some new clothes, she has been asking me for weeks and has finally made me arrange to go with her, so I will speak with you again later.'

Norak laughed at Voix's words, 'Yes, Voix, you can always rely on the woman of the house to spend your wealth, I wish you happy shopping,' he said with a chuckle.

Voix left and allowed Norak to carry on with his reading. As Voix left the room, Norak's eyes followed him until he had gone from the library.

As Kaleena was walking through the town where Roella lived, she saw a notice in a window of one of the shops, the notice read: **"CLOSING DOWN DUE TO**

FAMILY ILLNESS, SEE WITHIN FOR FURTHER DETAILS."

Kaleena stood and read the notice a second time and assessed the shop and thought it would be perfect for her weapons store. She had been thinking about what she was going to stock within it and considered adding not only firearms, but also archery equipment and crossbows of various designs. She'd also considered adding clothes of various types, on one side of the interior for the weapons and on the other side for adults clothing suitable for hunting and outdoor pursuits.

With a broad smile on her face she walked over to the shop and entered it. She looked around whilst the shop owner served a customer. The shop currently sold hardware and household utensils of various sorts. The woman paid for her new stewing pan and left. Kaleena viewed the shop owner. He looked to be about in his 40s and stood about five feet six with a stocky build and a round bulbous face and rosy cheeks, giving the impression he liked the outdoors. He sported a bald head and had a friendly smile, 'Yes, my dear, what can I do for you?' he asked in a very friendly voice.

Kaleena smiled at him, 'Well, Sir, I have noticed that you are closing your premises down due to family illness, I might be interested in buying it from you, but I hope your family illness is not too serious?' she asked with a friendly concern.

'It's my wife, she is riddled with bone problems and can't move around very well, I have decided to close my shop to spend more time with her.'

'I see, that is a very admirable choice and I am sure your wife is thankful for it. My name is Kaleena,

26

could you tell me when you hope to close your premises?'

'Well, Kaleena, My name is Ruffus and I would close it down as soon as I had a definite offer.'

Kaleena and Ruffus discussed a sale price and agreed that Kaleena would take over the shop in two weeks time.

They shook hands on the sale and Kaleena left the shop feeling happy that the next stage of her plan had been put into action. Her next two moves were to let Norak know about the shop and then contact her suppliers in her own town and arrange to have her stock delivered when her shop was ready.

Kaleena and Roella had already arranged to meet once a week in the Grewlers Tavern in the town and their meeting was the day after. She was keen to let her know so she could pass her news to her so Roella could let Norak know what she'd done so far.

<<<<< >>>>>

Roella walked into the Grewlers tavern where she had an arrangement to meet Kaleena. They had been meeting there for some time and no one suspected anything going on between them and the regulars had got to know them. One regular in particular was Jake, who had made the mistake of trying to force himself on Kaleena and found himself flying through the air with the greatest of ease as she threw him over her shoulder and then made him apologise or she would have broken his arm. By doing so, she had gained his respect and he kept away from her, and so did any other unwanted company.

Roella sat next to Kaleena and they gave each other a friendly hug as friends do and the barmaid brought her, her usual half tankard of beer, 'Good evening, Roella, how are you tonight?' Loren asked her.

'Roella nodded to her and smiled, 'I'm fine, thanks, ready for a rest and a drink and a chat with Kaleena.'

'I'll leave you to your conversation then,' Loren said and went back to the bar.

Kaleena smiled at Roella, 'I've got some great News for you to pass onto Norak. I have obtained a shop and will be moving into it in two weeks.'

'That's great news, Kaleena, he will be very pleased about that, when you get into it, I'm sure Norak will visit you, but very well disguised.'

'That will be good; we can then hope that we get some of the rebels coming to the shop asking for weapons. It will be too much of a temptation for them not to come and check it out.'

'Very true, Kaleena, things are coming together very well, but from what I understand from Norak, the rebels are beginning to accumulate in numbers, so we need to find out where they meet and who their top leader is.'

They talked and drank a few tankards of beer and then left together and eventually went back to their homes.

Roella walked into Norak's chamber with a tray of drinks for him, he was expecting a few of his councillors to discuss business for the town. Roella put the tray down, and looked at him and quietly said, 'Norak, I have news from Kaleena.'

He looked round the room to make sure no one was around, the room was clear, 'What is your news, Roella, good news I hope?' he asked.

'Yes, Norak, I met with Kaleena last night at the Grewlers Tavern, she has obtained a shop and will be opening up in two weeks. She is hoping that she will be contacted by the rebels soon after.'

'That's good news, Roella, keep me informed,' he said as three of his councillors walked through the entrance to his room.

Roella left them to discuss their business and was pleased she'd been able to tell Norak the news before anyone came.

The next two weeks passed quickly and Kaleena was pleased that at last, she had her shop and her stock of weapons was building, although not all of it had been delivered yet. Her Archery equipment was still on its way, but her clothing side was building up quite well and she had a variety of handguns and several rifle type weapons. She had a few crossbows and people were coming in and showing interest. Some were purchasing the odd gun and a few crossbows had been bought too by some of the locals, but she thought that they had nothing to do with the rebels, but word was slowly getting around about her shop.

<<<<< >>>>>

Scaroon was down a darkened alleyway speaking to a shadowy figure dressed in a dark cloak with a hood covering his head, 'Why have you called me here?' Scaroon asked the strange shadowy figure.

'Because there is a new shop opened across the way that is now selling guns and other useful weapons, take a look round it and see what is available, we need weapons of various types, even the crossbows are useful for killing from a distance and very accurately without any sound to attract attention,' he said in a whispery voice.

Scaroon nodded to the figure after finishing speaking to him, who then left him running down the rear of a building and disappeared into the night.

Scaroon walked the opposite way towards the street and came out under a street lamp and surreptitiously walked across the street and looked into the closed shop that was in semi darkness and planned to visit it the following day.

Scaroon walked into the weapons shop and looked around, he saw two people at the back of a long counter that were obviously there to serve customers. He observed them careful whilst they served a middle-aged man who had just bought a medium strain crossbow. He waited whilst looking closely at the weapons hanging from the walls.

As the other customer walked out, he heard a voice from behind him, 'Can I help you, Sir?' the voice asked.

He turned round and looked at the woman that had just spoken to him; she was a very attractive young woman and proffered a very nice smile, 'I was just observing your selection of armaments, I am considering starting a gun club and would need a selection of different weapons, would you be able to supply my needs?'

Kaleena was listening to the conversation between her shop assistant, Francesca and the tall thin man who was dressed in merchant's type clothing and sported a scar on his right cheek.

Francesca answered him, 'I'm sure we could accommodate you sir, so long as you give us time to get them from our suppliers. When would you want them, Sir?' she asked in a warm tone.

'I would have to consult my business partner first and tell him of the range you have, I will call and see you in two days and discuss the matter further.'

'Very well, Sir, we will look forward to helping you,' Francesca said with a smile as he walked out of the shop with a slight grin on his face as he looked at her and then glanced to Kaleena as he went through the door.

Kaleena watched his every move and wondered if he was her connection to the rebels, he looked the type and his scar reminded her of a typical rebel character. She knew she had to inform Roella about him and hoped to learn more about the gun club he claimed to be setting up. She looked at Francesca and said, 'Well, done, you handled him very well, I am quite keen to know more about where this gun club is going to be. When he comes in again, asked him very casually where he is setting it up and does he wish to have the guns and anything else he wants, delivered.'

Francesca smiled at Kaleena, she didn't know anything about why Kaleena had opened her shop, she was just grateful that she had been given the job of being her assistant. Up to the shop opening, Francesca didn't know Kaleena. Francesca smiled at her as a seed of a thought passed through her head, for the time being she kept the thought to herself.

Roella walked into the Grewlers tavern and hoped to see Kaleena there, however, this time Kaleena wasn't waiting for her. The barmaid, Loren brought Roella her usual Tankard of beer and said as she put the tankard down, 'Is Kaleena coming tonight? If she is, she's late.'

As Loren spoke her words, Kaleena came in the tavern door walking over to Roella and sat with her. Roella was concerned as she saw that Kaleena had a worried look on her face. Kaleena looked at Loren and said, 'I'll have my usual, please, Loren.'

Loren went to the bar and returned very quickly with Kaleena's tankard of beer, and left them to speak. Roella asked, 'What is it that bothers you, Kaleena, you have a look of worry on your face?'

Kaleena leaned closer to Roella, 'I think we have sparked off interest with the rebels, I'm sure that one of my customers who came in today is connected with them. He came in with the story he is going to set up a gun club, but I don't know where yet. However, he is coming back in two days to give us more details, I will then get to know where this gun club is going to be, but I have a feeling that the gun club could be where they are having their meetings.'

Two days later the man returned to the shop and started to browse around, while Kaleena and Francesca were serving another customer. The customer paid for the items he required and left the shop. Francesca then walks over to him.

'Good morning, sir, how nice to see you again, how can we help you?' Francesca asked him.

'Good morning, miss, yes I have decided that I will need twenty hand guns, five crossbows, six rifles and twelve long-swords and a variety of daggers,' he told her.

'Very good, Sir if you would like to come over to the counter we can get them ordered for you,' Francesca said with a smile and led him over to the counter where a display of various daggers and swords were displayed beneath the glass top.

Kaleena then spoke, 'When and where would you like the weapons delivered?' she asked, then quickly added, 'that is of course when we have taken delivery of them ourselves.'

The man looked at her with a strange expression on his face, 'I didn't know you had a delivery service, there's no notice of it in the window or on the premises,' he replied

'Oh, I'm sorry, Sir, we only decided to start one this week, but we haven't had time to get a sign made yet, our business is getting very busy, but we shall have one very soon,' Kaleena told him and sounding very convincing.

'Alright, miss, I'll need them in two days, if they have been delivered to you and you can deliver them to my gun club in the village of Banters Croft, it's called "*Rooks*", you can't miss it, it's the next building just after Banters Tavern at the end of the main street.

'Very well, sir, I will deliver them myself if that's agreeable with you,' Kaleena told him.

'I have no objections with that, I will meet you there the day after tomorrow if they arrive on time, if not, we will make further arrangements, but hopefully I will see you around 8:30am in two days time.' He paid for the weapons that he'd ordered and said good-bye and turned to leave the shop.

'Very well, sir until then, goodbye for now and thank you for your custom,' Kalenna said with a smile of satisfaction.

Norak was speaking to his councillors in the meeting room, 'We are trying to find a way to discover where the rebels are meeting and what their plans are.'

'How do you intend to do this, Norak,' asked Kalock.

'I'm not sure at this moment in time,' Norak said, knowing what he had already put into place, but wasn't going to tell them in order that no one could interfere or discover the truth and betray the Annarki and the Neanderthals.

At the end of the meeting Voix asks Norak if he could have a word in private. Norak took Voix to his private room to talk with him, 'So, what do you wish to ask me Voix?'

Voix looked at Norak questioningly, 'Norak, does this mean you've found someone to be our spy, but not telling the council?' Voix asked.

Norak was curious why Voix should ask this question of him, 'No, Voix, I haven't at this time, and even if I had, I wouldn't tell you or anyone else the plans so they could be ruined by anyone and turned against us.'

'That's true, Norak, I am in total agreement with you and thank you for taking the time to talk with me, I will go and carry on with my business, I'll see you later, bye for now,' Voix said and left Norak to deal with his own affairs.

'Ok, Voix, see you later.' Voix left none the wiser about what Norak was doing to find out who the rebel leader was.

Norak left the meeting room and went straight to his library to read a book and relax. Just as he sat down, Roella walked into the room, 'Can I speak to you, Norak it's important,' she said.

'Of course, Roella, please sit down, what can I do for you?' he asked her looking at her with a curious expression.

'Well, Norak, I have had word from Kaleena and she has told me that a man has been into the shop and bought some weapons from her and she thinks he might have some connection to the rebels.'

'Go on, Roella, I am intrigued to know more.'

'Well, the man has asked them to deliver the weapons to his gun club, which is called "Rooks" in the village of Banters Croft just up from Banters Tavern, they are taking the variety of weapons in a couple of days,' Roella told him.

'That's good news, Roella, thank you, could you bring me something to eat and a tankard of drulag please and we'll continue this conversation?' Norak asked her.

Roella left and moments later returned with a plate of sandwiches and a tankard of drulag.

'Thank you, Roella, please sit down, it would seem things are going to plan, this man who has bought the weapons could be a lead to who the Rebels are, we shall have to keep an eye on the situation,' Norak said, 'however, they haven't done anything yet to cause us to bring the authorities in to stop them. Before we do that, we have to have proof that this man and his friends are the rebels, it only looks like it at the moment, until we have solid proof we can't make a move.'

'That is true, Norak, but Kaleena feels there is something about him that makes her suspicious, but she is keeping a close eye on the situation and after she has delivered the weapons, we will know exactly where they work from, if they are the Rebels. I'll keep you informed as Kaleena tells me more information about them.'

'Very well, Roella, let's hope she is right about her suspicions. I'll let you get on with your work and we'll speak again soon.'

Roella left him and he settled down to read his book again, but was wondering if the man who has purchased the weapons is part of the rebels.

<<<<< >>>>>

Two days later, Kaleena had been able to get the weapons to take to the Rooks Gun Club. She and Francesca loaded up the wagon to take the weapons to Banters Croft. Shortly after they set off towards Traylers Bend, which led them to Banters Green and then on to Banters Croft, Kaleena said to Francesca, 'When we get there, keep your eyes peeled and try and see any signs that would suggest they are connected to the Rebels.'

'Rebels, what's this all about, Rebels? You have not mentioned this before, is there something I should know?' she asked Kaleena feeling a little in the dark.

'I'm sorry, Francesca, I should have told you and thought I had, but there is a group of rebels beginning to form that are trying to overrun the High Council, I am trying to find out about them so I can report their where-about of them to the head councillor. When I gave you the job at the shop, I knew you were innocent of the rebel rising against the High Council and meant to tell you before now, I'm sorry for that, but please keep this to yourself,' Kaleena asked her.

Francesca looked at Kaleena, 'Fear not, Kaleena, I will help you in any way I can, I don't want any disruption, I think the High Council do a great job of running our town.'

'That's good, Francesca, just follow my lead and agree with anything I say. I will tell you more when we get back to the shop. We only have our suspicions right now, we can't prove anything. It's possible that the Gun Club is a genuine concern for people to go and learn how to use the weapons. However, my gut feeling tells me that they are connected to the Rebel group in some way.'

'Yes, Kaleena, now you put it that way, I can see what you mean, we shall have to be very careful not to cast any suspicion on ourselves too, or we could be two of their next victims.'

Kaleena nodded as though agreeing with her as she steered the wagon onwards to Banter's Croft, 'Very good, Francesca, just play it cool and see what happens.'

Francesca and Kaleena were enjoying the ride through the local countryside as they got little opportunity to do so now they had the shop. Francesca turned to Kaleena and said, 'Kaleena, I am so excited about working with you in the shop. I'm really enjoying it,' Francesca said.

'I know what you mean, Francesca, it's wonderful, I would never have dreamed it could have taken off like it has.' Kaleena said.

'There's one thing that puzzles me Kaleena, now you have told me what you have about the rebels, this man we're delivering the weapons too, doesn't he strike you as a bit strange and that he is up to something more sinister than running a guns and weapons club? I think you could be right, and that he has something to do with the Rebels.'

'We shall have to wait and see, Francesca, and be very careful not to let on our thoughts, the man we have been dealing with could turn very nasty and cause us major problems, he gives me that kind of a feeling. We must keep an unsuspicious demeanour and just be friendly as though we know or suspect nothing.'

'Yes, Kaleena, I agree, we'll just drop them off where they want them and leave without asking any questions. Quite honestly, I would like to be there as shorter time as possible and get back to the shop.

On arriving, they were greeted by the man who came to the shop, 'Good morning, ladies, you both decided to come then?' he asked.

Kaleena smiled and looked back at him, 'Yes, we thought it such a lovely day and decided to take advantage and enjoy the ride in the countryside,' she said with a wide smile.

Scaroon looked at her with a smile and answered her, 'And why not, it's certainly a beautiful day,' he said, then looked at Francesca with an admiring look and gave her the impression she had taken his eye. She just smiled and said nothing.

Kaleena noticed Scaroon's glance at Francesca, and kept it in mind for later discussion with her and said, 'Where would you like us to drop them off for you, Sir?'

'If you follow me I will show you round to the rear of the building. I would like you to drop them off so we can put them on the back staging that leads into the armoury where we are keeping all weapons until needed for our clients.'

Scaroon led the way and Kaleena and Francesca followed him with the wagon they had brought the guns and bows on etc. Scaroon showed them the landing and Kaleena pulled the wagon up to the edge that made it easy to drag the boxes of equipment straight onto the back of the landing.

Kaleena and Francesca alighted from the wagon and walked to the rear to drop down the carts rear backboard so it was about level with the landing. All three of them walked up the wooden stairs and walked across the landing to the rear of the wagon, and began to slide and carry some of the boxes of weapons into the back of the building. Scaroon had already opened the rear doors ready to take delivery of his goods.

Kaleena and Francesca enter the building to discover a few practice targets and a smaller area with doors, which looks like they led to a selection of interlocking rooms. Kaleena and Frnacesca put the boxes down that they were carrying near the practice targets and then turned to return to drag off the boxes with the rifles in. However, before they got back to the wagon, Scaroon had already begun to drag the boxes of rifles in himself.

'Oh, Thank you Sir, but we could have managed,' she said to him smiling with a grateful expression.

'That's alright, ladies and thank you for being so prompt.'

'It's all part of the service, Sir, just let us know should you wish to add to your armoury, we would be glad to supply you,' Kaleena said with a smile.

Francesca looked at Scaroon and saw him looking at her again with a look of admiration; she felt a little wary but just smiled back at him.

At that moment, six men walked in from the rear of the shop to join them. Scaroon saw them and said, 'These gentlemen are some of my members, we will be trying out your weapons later, and if we are satisfied with them, as I'm sure we will be, I may be purchasing more from you soon,' Scaroon said with a smile.

'Why, thank you, kind Sir, we are glad to be of service and we hope that these weapons are satisfactory to your needs,' Kaleena said.

'Thank you, ladies, now if you don't mind we need to get on with our business, so good bye for now and thank you once again,' he said as he began to close the rear doors to the building.

Very well, Sir, thank you and good day,' Kaleena said as she stirred up the horse and set off back to the shop.

As they were riding back, Kaleena looked at Francesca with a smile, 'I think that our client, whatever his name is, has taken a shine to you, Francesca. How do you feel about that?'

Francesca looked across to Kaleena, 'Well, it came over very obvious to me and in spite of his roguish looks, he has a strange appeal to him, I don't find him offensive in a bad way, in fact, I could find myself getting to know him better.'

Kaleena looked at Francesca with a little shock on her face, 'Are you saying that you would accept him becoming friendlier with you?'

'Yes, Kaleena, but my motives are not intended to fall in love with the man, but I could enjoy his company, and it would also work for both of us if he has anything to do with the Rebels. But if that is the case, we have to find a way so I can meet with them in one of their meetings.'

Kaleena smiled at her, 'Well, Francesca, you're not just a pretty face are you, I like what you are saying, but what happens if you do get very close and you do fall in love with him,' she asked her with concern.

'Well, if that should happen, I will have to be very careful and see how things go. We shall have to work that one out as it happens, or doesn't happen. We are only speculating at the moment aren't we?'

Chapter Four

Barook's Choice:

Shnark looked at Jarako and said, 'You need to get Sheraba to come and help you, she is your main assistant,' Snark looked at one of the security guards and said, 'we need Jarako's assistance, can you arrange for her to come here and help us. She is called, Sheraba.'

There were four security guards with them in the laboratory, Ashtuk made sure they wouldn't be able to do anything just in case they were Greylon spies with a good story. One of the guards went to the secure room where the rest of the Greylon rebels were waiting. The guard walked into the room and said, 'Who is Sheraba, you are needed by your scientist, Jarako, follow me.'

Sheraba stood up from her seat and began to follow the guard to the laboratory. As she entered, Shnark looked at her and said, 'I want you to help Jarakoo with the new weapon designs, it's imperative that this new weapons works first time, if it doesn't we are all dead meat.'

Sheraba looked at Shnark with a scared look. 'Why has it got to be done now, I thought we were hoping to go to the Annaki planet and show the leader?'

Shnark looked at her and answered, 'The leader of the Annaki has spoken to us on the screen in the control room and made it quite clear that we have to draw out the plans for the new weapon and prove it to him before we get anywhere nearer going onto their planet. Barook himself is coming aboard to see the plans, and he is not a man to upset, he is very trigger happy and wouldn't hesitate to vaporise us if we get it wrong, so make sure you and Jarako get it right.'

'Very well,' she looked at Jarako, 'in that case we had better get started.

They walked across to what looked like a drawing board that was positioned on top of a control stand with various controls for drawing technical drawings. Shnark walked with them and asked Jarako if he knew how to use this type of drawing board. Jarako said he did and Shnark sighed with relief.

Jarako looked at Shnark and said, 'Go over to the seats by the observation window and let me and Sheraba get on with this drawing.'

Shnark did as Jarako had told him and went to the observation window and began to stare into space. Jarako and Sheraba began to draw the new weapon designs on the techno-board drawing surface. They worked without stopping for the next three hours and eventually completed it.

Shnark, we have finished, come and have a look at it.'

Shnark got up and went to view what they had done. He was impressed at the detail of the drawing, but didn't understand what it all meant or how it worked. 'It looks amazing and technical but how the hell does it work?' he asked staring at the drawing.

Jarako looked at Shnark and said pointing his finger at the drawing at the rear end of the weapon. 'Well, the collected agitated Neutron particles are injected into the particle transformer at the rear, they are then energised by the magnetic transducer ray which agitates them further and makes them more powerful. They then pass through the photon magnifier and into the projection unit. Here they become powered by Nuformic plasma gas that creates a high intensive heat beam, which is projected at one hundred times the original power of the neutrons and is aimed through the three outlets at the front of the ejection ports at the target. The destruction force is equivalent to one million photon light beams that will obliterate anything in its path, by vaporising whatever it comes into contact with. I think that Barook will be impressed. If we set it to a lower power to work in a short room area, say in the hold of the ship and aim it at some kind of metal target, such as an empty food storage container, it will destroy and vaporise the container in a fraction of a second.' Jarako explained.

Shnark just looked in awe at the device drawing and said, 'My question is, we can't demonstrate the weapon unless the Annaki have the materials to construct it.'

'Yes, Shnark, I know this, we need to speak with Barook again to ask him for the materials, and then we can demonstrate the weapon to him as I have suggested.'

'Very well, we can ask and hope Barook is agreeable.' Snark looked at the security guards and asked, 'Can you please put us through to the ships control room so we can talk to Ashtuk, we need to ask for the materials to make the new weapon.'

The guard went to the monitor on the wall and pressed a few buttons, moments later they saw Ashtuk appear on the screen, 'Yes, Bargo, what is it you wish?' he asked the guard in a stern voice.

Bargo looked straight at Ashtuk and answered, 'The two scientists have finished the drawing for the new weapon and wish to speak with you.'

'Very well, bring them to the monitor and let them speak.'

Bargo looked across to Jarako and Sheraba, 'You can come to the screen and speak with Ashtuk,' he said abruptly.

Without hesitation they went to the screen and looked at Ashtuk, 'Ashtuk, we have finished the plan drawings for the new weapon we have developed, but we need the materials to build it and some production tools to make some of them, until we have these things, we cannot proceed with it,' he said hoping there wouldn't be a problem.

Ashtuk looked at them and said, 'Let me see the drawings on the drawing unit, there is a button that will send the drawing to the control room computer screen, it just says, "Transmit", press it and I will look them over and then I'll see about your materials and equipment to produce the required parts. When I'm happy with the drawings, I will come back to you. Send a list with the drawings of what you will need, our engineering deck will have all the equipment you'll need and probably the materials, unless there is something special that we can't supply. In that case, you will have to wait until we can get them from our planet,' he told them.

'Very well, Ashtuk,' Jarako said and went across to the drawing board and added a list of the materials they would need to build the weapon. Having done this, he press the button, "transmit" and it suddenly disappeared from the drawing board and moments later appeared on the large monitor in the control room.'

Ashtuk looked at it with his science officer and scrutinised it trying to work out how it would work, they were lost as to what mechanism worked the weapon and decided that he would need to get the three Greylons to come and explain it to him.

He went to the transmission control unit and pressed the transmission button for the Ships laboratory. He saw Jarako and Sheraba on the screen and they were waiting for his transmission to them, Ashtuk looked at them and said, 'All three of you come to the control room and explain how this weapon works, I need to know before we let you proceed.'

Bargo, the guard was listening to Ashtuk's voice and as soon as the screen went blank, he escorted the three Greylons to the control room.

As they entered, Ashtuk took them across to the monitor that had an expanded view on of the weapon drawings. Ashtuk looked at them and said, 'Will one of you scientists explain to me how this weapon works, we have checked your material list and we have all you need on board.'

Jarako looked at the large monitor and began to explain to Ashtuk how it worked, Jarako pointed his finger at the drawing at the rear end of the weapon. 'Well, the collected agitated Neutron particles are injected into the particle transformer at the rear, they are then energised by the magnetic transducer ray which agitates them further and makes them more powerful. They then pass through the photon magnifier and into the projection unit. Here they become powered by Nuformic plasma gas that creates a high intensive heat beam, which is projected at one hundred times the original power of the neutrons and is aimed through the three outlets at the front of the ejection ports, at the target. The destruction force is equivalent to one million photon light beams that will obliterate anything in its path by vaporising it. If we set it to a lower power to work in a short room area, say in the hold of the ship and aim it at some kind of metal target, such as an empty food storage container, it will destroy and vaporise the container in a fraction of a second.' Jarako explained.

Ashtuk looked at Jarako and almost smiled, but just made it a satisfactory look at him, 'Very well, Jarako, the guard will take you to our engineering deck and you can begin to build your weapon. Just make sure it works when you have completed it as you have to convince Barook after you have convinced me, and as you now know, he is not an easy one to please,' Ashtuk said.

Jarako looked at Ashtuk confidently, 'Don't worry, Ashtuk, it will work. We will get started right away.'

'Very well, let me know as soon as you have built your weapon and transported it down to the cargo bay. We shall find you a target to aim it at, but make sure you don't make any mistakes, if the beam breeches the outer hull, you'll be sucked out into space.'

Jarako suddenly had an idea, 'Ashtuk, I have had a better idea to demonstrate the weapon, we could send a small unwanted droid or something out into space and use the weapon to destroy it as though it was an invading ship.'

Ashtuk was impressed by the idea, 'Mm, you're not just a clever scientist are you, Jarako, that is an excellent idea, we will do that, we have several unwanted droids and probes we can use. Now go and build this weapon and impress me,' Ashtuk told him.

Kaleena and Francesca enjoyed their ride back to the shop and discussed the situation in more detail and Kaleena was beginning to like Francesca's idea about a relationship with Scaroon.

As they approached the shop, they saw a strange character standing outside as though waiting for them to return. Kaleena looked at him and said to Francesca, 'I think I know who that man is and his disguises get better, it's Norak.'

They pulled up outside the shop and Kaleena looked down at him as he looked up at her and smiled, 'Hello, ladies, I would like to discuss buying some of your weapons,' he said with a smile and knowing that Kaleena and Francesca had recognised him, however, no one else on the street did, which was his intentions.

Kaleena played along with him, 'Very well, Sir, my friend here will let you in whilst I take the wagon round the back of the shop and put our horse in the stable, he's done his work well for today,' she said with a smile at Norak.

Francesca climbed down from the wagon, and went towards the shop door, she opened it, and she and Norak went inside. Kaleena would join them shortly and come into the shop from the rear entrance.

'Was your trip to the Gun Club a worthwhile one, Francesca?' he asked her.

'Yes, Norak, it went very well, I have a feeling we shall be hearing from Scaroon again very soon.'

At that moment, Kaleena came in from the rear of the shop and joined them. 'Ah, Kaleena, Francesca has told me that everything went well with your delivery and that you expect Scaroon to buy more weapons,' he said.

Kaleena smiled at Norak, 'Yes, Norak, I think we shall be seeing him again soon, he was well impressed with his delivery and we also saw some of the men from the gun club. Scaroon said they were club members, but I got a strong feeling that they were some of the rebels. Time will tell, we shall have to see what happens from now on.'

'What is the Gun Club like? Do you think it could be their headquarters for their meetings? They must have somewhere to meet and that would be an ideal front for such an organisation as the rebels.'

Kaleena looked at him and grinned, 'To answer your first question, Norak, the Gun Club is set up very efficiently and suited very well for the business he proposes to have, and secondly, the building is very spacious and ideal for rebel meetings. However, we have a potential secret weapon,' she said looking over to Francesca, 'Francesca could be the link to the internal movements of the Rebels organisation. It seems that Scaroon has taken a shine to her and she is quite willing to go along with his charms.'

Norak looked across to Francesca and was a little concerned, but at the same time he was intrigued at the idea, 'Francesca, you could be tempting fate on dangerous ground. If Scaroon is the Rebel leader, and found out that you are a spy in their midst, you could find yourself in a very dangerous situation.'

Francesca smiled at him, 'Don't worry, Norak, Kaleena is teaching me the art of hand to hand combat and I'm learning very quickly. She is a very good instructor.'

'Yes, Francesca, I know that and I'm glad you are learning the fighting arts, they are important to learn in these times of rebellion and unrest. However, be careful not to let on you are helping find out where the rebels are meeting. You have no idea what Scaroon would do if he knew you were helping me. Take great care all the time you are around him.'

Francesca smiled warmly at Norak, 'I will be careful, Norak, I promise you, but I should soon find out if Scaroon is involved with the rebels and I'll let you know through Kaleena and your daughter when I find anything out.'

'Very well, Francesca, but I will worry about you and hope nothing happens to you. I will leave now before I'm missed at home. I will look forward to hearing some news as soon as you get to know something. Good day to you both,' he said and left the shop and mounted his horse and set off up the street at a gentle trot.

As Norak left Kaleena's shop, Kaleena looked at Francesca and asked, 'Francesca, are you sure about getting involved with Scaroon? Norak was right when he said you could find yourself in great danger, even though you are becoming very good at the fighting arts.'

'We'll have to wait and see, but if I see any danger coming my way, I will make a move to get out of it very quickly. I think that Scaroon is the leader of the rebels; I noticed how he ordered the men about at the Gun Club, he is a natural leader and he is very organised too, I like that in a man, I think I will get along fine with him when we actually get together. I have a feeling he will be calling at the shop very soon, and not just to order more weapons, he will be coming to see me,' she said with a wide smile.

Kaleena chuckled at her, 'You are infatuated with him aren't you, but be careful, Francesca, I don't want anything to happen to you.'

'Don't worry, Kaleena, I will be alright, I'm, quite intrigued to see what he is like when not with his men or rebels, if that's what they are. Let's just wait and see how things turn out.

Kaleena nodded to her and gave a sigh, 'Okay, we'll soon find out, I think you will see Scaroon quicker than you think, I just feel he will be seeing you very soon. Meanwhile, would you like to join Roella and I tonight at the Grewlers Tavern, it would be nice to have an evening together. You don't live far from the tavern do you?' she asked her.

'No, I'm only about five minutes walk from it, so it won't take me long to get home when it's time to go.'

Later that day, Kaleena and Roella were in the Grewlers tavern and hoping that Francesca would join them. They were just ordering their second tankard of ale when Francesca walked in the door and saw them sitting in the corner of the room. She began to walk over to them, but as she walked past one of the customers, he put his hand on her hip and tried to pull her to him. She promptly turned and chopped his shoulder on the top attacking one of the nerves and he quickly retreated his hand, she turned to him and said, 'Try that again and I'll break your arm you lecherous bastard.'

He looked up at her and growled and she carried on towards Kaleena and Roella. Kaleena was watching as she chopped the man who tried it on with her, 'Well done, Francesca, you were well able to cure his assault on you, he is a pain in the butt, he once tried it on with me and I put his arm into a very painful lock and he never tried it again.'

'Well, Kaleena, that's thanks to you and your teaching, he might think twice next time.'

Francesca smiled and answered, 'If he tries it again, I'll break his arm, not chop it.'

Kaleena and Roella laughed at her comment and Francesca sat with them at the table. Kaleena went to the bar and fetched her a tankard of ale and she drank from it eagerly being quite thirsty.

Roella asked Francesca, 'Are you enjoying working with Kaleena, Francesca?' she asked.

'Yes, Roella, it's fun and sometimes gets exciting. I take it that Kaleena has told you about our trip to the Gun Club today?' she asked.

'Yes, she has, she's also told me about your possible entanglement with the Gun Club owner. Be very careful, it could get very dangerous, especially if he has anything to do with the rebels.'

Francesca smiled at her, 'Worry not, Roella, I am well aware of the possibilities and dangers, but I will enjoy getting to know Scaroon, I think we will get on just fine.'

'I spoke with Norak earlier today, he is very concerned for you and hopes you don't get hurt, or worse,' Roella added.

Kaleena then said, 'I think that Francesca will be alright, if she gets close to Scaroon, he will not want to see her get hurt, he could turn out to be very useful.'

Francesca smiled at them both, 'I hope he doesn't take too long in coming to see me at the shop, I am quite keen to see him away from his Gun Club and meet him alone.'

Kaleena smiled at her, 'I think secretly that you quite fancy Scaroon, but move with caution, you don't know what he's like yet, be careful.'

'I will, Kaleena, don't worry, I will be alright.'

Chapter Five

Testing the weapon:

Jarako and Sheraba got to work on the weapon and began to engineer the different parts from what the ship had in its large collection of technological equipment. Most of the components had to be changed and engineered to fit the new weapon's device, but their skill was excellent and efficient and they were soon assembling the new laser type weapon.

Shnark watched them at a distance without disturbing them and was curious as to how the weapon would work, even though Jarako had tried to explain it to him. He hoped for everyone's sake that the weapon would work when completed.

He cautiously walked over to Jarako and Sheraba, 'Is everything going to your plans?' he asked in a tentative voice.

Jarako looked at him with a smile, 'Of course it is, don't worry, Shnark, it will work and do as we say it will, Barook will be pleased with the result. I can assure you that we won't be vaporised,' he said with confidence.

Shnark knew that Jarako was a brilliant scientist and so was Sheraba, but he feared for their lives if there was just one problem. He wanted Barook to accept them and allow them to join them as allies, even though they were only small in number as Greylon dissenters.

Eventually after working without stopping, Jarako and Sheraba finished the weapon and it was ready for firing. They turned to Shnark and smiled, 'There you are, Shnark, it's ready to be installed into the best place for it. We can now let Ashtuk know we've done.'

Shnark looked over at the two guards who were talking to each other by the door of the engineering unit. 'Guards, the weapon is ready to install and test, can you let Astuk know we are ready to demonstrate it.'

One of the guards went to the screen and contacted Ashtuk. Moments later, Ashtuk appeared on the monitor, 'Yes, have they finished the weapon,' he asked in an impatient voice.

The guard looked straight into Ashtuk's eyes, 'Yes, Captain, it is ready to install, Jarako suggests it be installed at the front of the ship and be made ready to test.'

'Very well, I will get our ships engineers down to come and help install it ready for its first trial, I hope it works, or there will be trouble,' he said.

Shnark, Jarako and Sheraba could hear what Ashtuk said and came to the screen, Jarako said, 'I can assure you that it will work, Ashtuk.'

'We will soon see, I have been informed by Barook that he is on his way to see it working. My engineers are going to help you install it at the front of the ship ready to test. Get it done as quickly as you can.'

'We will Ashtuk, we will,' Shnark answered him.

Over the next hour, the ships engineers, with Jarako and Sheraba's help, they installed the new weapon in its designated place and were ready to test it. A control panel had been installed in the control room so the weapon could be fired from the bridge, and Jarako, Sheraba and Shnark were taken to the Bridge to see it tested for the first time. Jarako and Sheraba were confident, but Shnark was a little apprehensive, he had taken Barook's threat serious and knew they would be vaporised if the weapon didn't work.

Ashtuk looked at the three Greylons and said, 'Right, here we go, let's try it out.' He turned to the front monitor that looked out into space directly in front of the ship. 'Release the defective probe and direct it to the front of the ship.'

Moments later, they saw a small craft appear from the lower section of the Annarkian craft. Jarako was at the controls to fire the weapon, Ashtuk said, 'Aim and fire, Jarako, and pray it works.'

Jarako directed the weapon at the projected craft that was the defective probe, he waited until the probe was in the centre of the weapon's sights and fired the beam. There was a sudden and slight vibration as the beam's powerful projection was seen heading towards the probe at a distance in front of the ship. It all happened in seconds, although it seemed to take ages with anticipation. The beam hit the probe, and it was immediately vaporised and vanished into nothingness as though there was nothing there, it was gone. The weapon worked.

For the first time since coming aboard, they saw Ashtuk smile, 'This is amazing, Greylons, Barook will be pleased with you. You have done well,' he said.

Shnark, Jarako and Sheraba sighed with relief at Ashtuk's words, especially Shnark who went to his two comrades and shook their hands, 'Well done, my friends, you have served us well.'

Ashtuk looked over to his two guards standing by the door to the control room, 'Guards, take these men to the refectory so they can eat and drink, they have proved their alliance to our people. Their friends can now join them too.'

Shnark, Jarako and Sheraba followed the two guards and they were taken to the refectory so they could eat and drink freely. When all their friends joined them, they were all pleased to see their comrades who had saved their skins..

After eating and refreshing themselves, they relaxed and talked together about what was to come. A short time after, Ashtuk came to them, 'Shnark, Jarako and you Sheraba are required on the bridge. Barook has arrived and is awaiting a demonstration of your new weapon.'

Shnark, Jarako and Sheraba stood up and followed Ashtuk and the two guards to the control room. As they walked in, they saw Barook standing by the forward monitor with his back to them.

Shnark, Jarako and Sheraba came to a standstill and waited for Barook to turn to them and speak. It seemed ages before Barook turned to look at them. He stared at them deep into their eyes without any expression on his face. He looked the three Greylons up and down and then looked at Ashtuk, 'Ashtuk, you say that their weapon actually works?'

'Yes, my Lord, it is what they say it is,' Ashtuk answered Barook.

Barook looked back at Shnark, Jarako and Sheraba, 'It seems you have proven yourselves, now I will have you demonstrate it to me also, I want to be impressed,' he said without any emotion in his voice.

Ashtuk gave the order for the second defective probe to be launched forward of the ship. Jarako went to the control panel of the weapon and began to aim the beam at the probe that had just shown itself. Moments later, Jarako pushed the firing button and the beam shot like lightning at the probe and vaporised it as it had done with the first one.

Barook just watched and saw the probe vanish into space as though it never existed. He turned back to the three Greylons and said, 'I am impressed, but I understand that your people have already got this weapon?' he asked.

Jarako answered Barook's question, 'Yes, my Lord Barook, but we have a device that can detect when it is going to be fired, it shows up on the targeting screen, just here,' he said as he pointed to the area that showed when the Greylons were going to fire their weapons.

So what do you want in return, but before you tell me, I want you to show my engineers how to build this weapon so it can be installed into all our war-ships.'

Shnark quickly said, 'We only wish to join you and serve you, my Lord.'

Barook quickly shot a glance at Shnark, 'Why is it so important that you join our people, I am still unsure about your reasons?' he asked.

Shnark thought carefully before he answered Barook, knowing his sinister character by now, 'Well, my Lord, we don't agree with the action of our people wanting to take over the Thaldernian planet. All they want are the resources it has, when they have used the Neanderthals as slaves to extract what they want, they will slaughter them without mercy. We do not wish to see that happen. The giving of this weapon and the new *Tachyon drive* is our way of proving our sincerity and allegiance to you.'

Barook looked at Shnark and nodded, 'Very well, but how long will it take to build and install this new *Tachyon drive* in to our ships?'

Shnark knew that he had Barook's attention and knew they had convinced him that they were genuine about helping the Annaki. 'My Lord Barook, we would need a larger space than this ship to build such drives, that is why we need to go to your planet and use the technology you have to build them. We can work alongside your engineers and teach them how to make the new Tachyon drive engines. We can begin as soon as we can get to your planet.'

Barook looked deeply at Shnark as though reading his mind, although he couldn't, he felt that Shnark was serious about helping them build the new Tachyon drive engines. 'Very well, we will take you and your people to our planet and allow you to build the new drives for our ships, but I give you fair warning, one move to destroy our people and the planet and you will be destroyed immediately, do you understand?' he said looking at all three Greylons.'

Shnark looked at him without any hesitation and said, 'Yes, my Lord, but you will see that we are truly wanting to help you.'

'You had better be sure, otherwise, you know what to expect,' Barook said and then looked at Ashtuk, 'Ashtuk, see that these Greylons are taken to my ship and shown them to their quarters, then return back to your normal duties.'

Ashtuk didn't question Barook's order and immediately they were taken to Barook's ship to await their trip back to Annaki.

62

Francesca kept watching the man who had tried to drag her to him, she noticed he was watching her and became very conscious of him. Kaleena had noticed that she kept looking at the man and knew the man to be a rogue and could be very argumentative.

'Francesca, just ignore the man, he's just trying to distract you and annoy you, you could deal with him if he gets clever without any problem, but I don't think he'll try it on with you again,' Kaleena said to her.

'I hope not, or I'll crack his skull with something very hard.'

Kaleena laughed at her answer and they continued chatting between themselves and ignored the annoying man.

Francesca stood up and noticed that the man who was bothering her earlier had left, she sighed with relief that he had gone. 'I'll be going now, I will see you tomorrow at the shop, Kaleena and I'll see you again soon, Roella, goodnight,' she said as she left the Tavern.

As she walked past the side alleyway that was by the side of the tavern, Francesca felt someone grab he from behind and pull her into the alleyway and held her tight from behind her. She tried to elbow him to his chest but it had no effect on him. He was very strong and she thought quickly as to what she was going to do next. She was about to back kick him to his shin when she felt the man let go of her. She quickly turned round ready to deliver another blow when she saw a man in dark clothing with his hand around the man's neck and sporting a sharp dagger type knife that she recognised as one of the knives from the shop. She saw the man slit the assailant's throat and watched him gurgled in his blood as he fell to the floor dead.

She then looked at the man dressed in the dark cloak as he uncovered his head, she saw it was Scaroon. She sighed with relief, 'Thank you, Scaroon, but what are you going to do with the man?'

'I'm going to leave him here, no one has seen us and will think he has been mugged for his money, it happens quite a lot. I know this man and he is not well liked, anyone of a dozen men would like him out of the way, including me,' he whispered to her.

'We need to go right now,' she said.

'Yes, we must, where were you going at this time of night?'

'I am going home, I only live a few streets away,' she told him.

Scaroon smiled at her and said, 'Forgive me, Miss Francesca, but I insist on seeing you get home safely.'

Francesca didn't argue the matter, and went with Scaroon as he held her hand and led her down the back of the alleyway and away from the tavern. When they got into the street away from where they had left the dead man, and could walk freely, Scaroon said, 'Where had you been, it's very late?'

I have just left Kaleena and her sister in the tavern; we met for a little social evening and a friendly chat.'

'I take it Kaleena is the woman who owns the Gun shop, she is a very clever woman and has a good business there.'

'Yes, it is, I enjoy working for her, she is very kind and knows her weapons.'

'I will be coming to see your friend again soon, my gun club is becoming very popular and I will need more guns and crossbows, they seem to be the most popular along with the bows and arrows.'

'That's good, Scaroon, we can certainly supply all you want. But tell me, why were you around the alleyway tonight, although I'm glad you were,' she asked.

Scaroon smiled at her, 'I had just left a friend of mine after discussing a little business, I saw Marcus, the man who attacked you, and wondered why he was lingering down the alleyway. When I saw him grab you, I came to his rear and slit his throat. He won't be missed by many people.'

Francesca smiled at him and suddenly felt very safe in Scaroon's company. As they walked, she felt an affinity towards him and didn't mind when he rested his right hand on her shoulders.

'I live just around the corner here, would you like to have a drink with me before taking your leave?' she asked him.

Scaroon was a little surprised at a lovely young lady asking him such a question, but didn't argue, 'Yes, I would like that, thank you.'

Francesca led him up the stairs to her home, which was above a bakers shop. As they went up the side stairs, Scaroon suddenly stopped and took in a deep smell through his nose, 'How I love the smell of fresh baked bread, it has to be one of the most wonderful smells in the world,' he said.

Francesca laughed a little at him and asked, 'Would you like some for your supper, the baker always leaves me a fresh loaf when he bakes his first batch, it is there by my door,' she said pointing to a small package wrapped in waterproof paper, just in case it rained.

'That would be very welcome, I am a little hungry, thank you yet again.'

Francesca smiled at him warmly, 'It's the least I can do, you saved me from a fate worse than death tonight and I am ever in your debt.'

As they got to the top of the stairs, Francesca turned and looked at Scaroon straight in his eyes, Scaroon couldn't help himself and bent towards her and kissed her, she responded agreeable to his actions and they kissed quite passionately.

When they parted, Scaroon said, 'Please forgive me, Francesca, I just couldn't help myself, you are a very beautiful lady.'

Francesca smiled at him, 'You don't have to apologise, I liked your actions and enjoyed your kiss. Let's go in where it's warmer and I'll make you a drink and cut you some fresh bread and with homemade butter.'

'You are too kind, I think we shall get on very well, I would like to see you again sometime,' he said to her.

'I would like that, Scaroon, let's take it one step at a time, first a drink, then the bread and see where we go from there,' she said with more meaning in her words than were said out loud.

Chapter Six

Progress:

Kaleena smiled at Francesca as she walked into the shop, Francesca looked at Kaleena standing behind the counter, 'Last night was very interesting, do you remember that man who was staring at me and tried it on,' she asked,

Yes, Francesca, what about him?'

'Well, when I went out to go home, he grabbed me and pulled me into the alleyway by the side of the tavern. I tried to elbow him in the stomach, but it had no effect. I was just about to smash his shins with the heel of my shoe when suddenly he let go and fell to the floor. When I turned round, I saw Scaroon there; he had slit the man's throat and killed him without batting an eyelid. He then took my hand and we left the man in the alleyway.'

Kaleena looked in horror at what Francesca had told her, 'Are you alright, Francesca?' Kaleena asked her with concern.

'Yes, I'm alright, thanks to Scaroon, he had seen the man lingering around the alleyway and watched him to see what he was up to. When he saw him grab me, he attacked him and killed him, and with one of the knives, he bought from this shop. He told me he was just going home after meeting one of his friends. I was so grateful for his help, although I think I would have dealt with the stupid man, had Scaroon not have turned up. He walked me home to make sure I was alright.'

'That was very kind of him, did he tell you anything about himself, or did you do all the talking?' Kaleena asked with a grin.

Francesca blushed a little and smiled, as though she was a little embarrassed. 'Well, we talked a lot about being careful when I go home from anywhere as he thought I was easy prey to not nice men who would want to take advantage of me, and he talked about the gun club and how well it was doing, and that he would be coming for more guns and other weapons very soon.'

Kaleena grinned at her, 'Is that all he spoke about?'

'Well he walked me to my apartment and came in for a drink and a slice or two of freshly baked bread from the bakery downstairs. I have to confess, he stayed for the night, he is really a nice man and a gentleman, even though he looks a little rough on the outside. I asked him where he got the scar from, on his face; he told me that it was in a knife fight when he defended a lady from being assaulted in a market place somewhere.'

Kaleena smiled at her and asked, 'Did he say anything about the rebels or give any hint of them at all?'

'No, he never mentioned anything about them, we might be wrong about him and that his gun club might be a genuine business. I get the feeling he is quite a wealthy man, but I have no idea where he got his money from,' Francesca told her.

'Mm, so he spent the night with you, I'm surprised you weren't late for work,' Kaleena said with a broad smile.

Francesca laughed at Kaleena's comment, 'In actual fact, Kaleena, he had to be up early himself to get back to his gun club, he said he was expecting some new members and had to be there to meet them early.

'Well, Francesca, you didn't waste any time getting to know him, I take it, it was mutual and agreeable with you?' Kaleena said with a wide grin.

Francesca laughed at her again, 'Oh yes, he was very agreeable and has lots of stamina,' she said grinning.

'I'm not going to ask any more, other than are you seeing him again soon?'

'Yes, he is coming to see me tonight; I'm going to cook him a homemade meal. It seems he lives on his own and doesn't really eat well.'

'Kaleena smiled warmly, 'Be careful, Francesca, he could be dangerous if you ask too many questions, chose your words carefully when talking with him.'

'I will, Kaleena, don't worry, but I have to admit, I hope he isn't connected with the rebels, I could get very close to him.'

'I think you already have, if your demeanour has anything to do with it, you're like a spring chicken this morning. Be sure to keep me informed about his background activities, what you do otherwise is your affair.'

'Alright, will do.'

Francesca was in her small kitchen in her apartment and preparing the meal she was cooking Scaroon, she knew he was due to get to her very soon now that it was dark. She had become very fond of him very quickly and after he had stopped with her the night before, she was already intimate with him and was growing to like him very much. She was preparing a steak pie, homemade, with a variety of vegetables.

She heard a knock at her door and knew it would be Scaroon. She put her cloth down she was using to move a pan over to the back of her stove and went to the door. As she opened it, she saw Scaroon smiling widely at her and he walked in and gave her a passionate kiss, 'Hello, Francesca, I've been looking forward to coming tonight all day, what are you cooking? It smells delicious.'

She leaned back from him slightly as he was still holding her to him, 'I'm cooking homemade steak pie with vegetables.'

'That sounds good, I haven't had homemade pie for years, you are really spoiling me, I think I just might fall in love with you,' he said with a big grin on his face.

He let her go and she said, 'Mm, we'll have to see what happens, Scaroon, but the idea is good,' she said taunting him with a smile.

He laughed at her and walked into the room where she had laid the table ready for their meal. Before he could say anything she asked, 'Did you get many new members for your club this morning? You said you were expecting more members before you left me.'

'Yes, we had eight new members, the membership is growing very well, we shall be needing more new weapons very soon if the membership continues to increase as it is, I didn't think it would become as popular as it has.'

'Oh, that's good, I'm sure Kaleena will be pleased to hear that, the weapon's shop is becoming very popular too and more people are coming from out of town, it seems word is spreading very well about us.'

'I think it could be because of the gun club too, we are telling everyone we know about Kaleena's shop, so that will have helped her business too. She has made it easier for people to get guns, bows, and other weapons without having to travel too far to other big towns.'

'Yes, I suppose that's true,' she said.

Francesca served up the meals on two large plates and she placed them on the table. They began eating and Scaroon was obviously enjoying his treat of Steak Pie. He cleared the plate and didn't leave a morsel.

Francesca smiled at him as he wiped his plate with a crust of bread, 'I take it you enjoyed that, Scaroon?' she asked.

He sat across from her holding his enlarged and full stomach resting his hands on it, 'Francesca, that was amazing, your pie was second to none, I thought it was incredible, you are a great cook, I think I will definitely fall in love with you,' he said giving Francesca a big smile.

Francesca laughed at him, 'Scaroon, you are just a big charmer, how can anyone fall in love with someone just because they have just had homemade pie cooked for them?' she asked with a loving smile.

Scaroon grinned at her with a cheeky expression, 'Francesca I fancied you the first time I saw you in the shop. When you came with Kaleena to deliver my guns and weapons, I saw you again and liked you even more, I'm so happy we have come together as we have, I haven't had a woman in my life for many years,' he told her.

Francesca looked at him with a loving stare and realised that he was being serious, 'Scaroon, what brought you to this area, your voice would suggest you come from further south?'

Scaroon stood up, took her by the hand, and led her over to the long couch she had that faced the fire. When they were comfortable, He looked at her seriously and said, 'I came to this area because of my brother. It was in this town you live in that my brother was murdered. I intend to find who did it, and finish him or them off as I did with the man who attacked you. I decided that I would start a gun club to see if I could attract the man or men that killed him, to join. Before I came here, no one knew me, so I began the gun club for that reason.'

'Is that the only reason you came here, Scaroon, I can understand you wanting revenge for your brother, but you'll have to be careful that the man or men that killed your brother doesn't find out who you really are, or they might want to kill you too.'

'I am very well aware of this, Francesca, but I am keeping my past to myself and telling everyone a different story about me and why I am here, once I have found my brother's killer or killers, I will be satisfied and will serve them their same justice.'

'But will you stay here when you have sought your revenge?' she asked him not knowing what he would say.

'Well, I had planned to get my revenge and then disappear and be gone, but I didn't expect to meet you, you could change my mind if we become closer, I would like too,' he said smiling at her and looking deep into her beautiful dark brown eyes.

74

Francesca leaned over to him and kissed him passionately and they eventually finished up in her bed until the morning.

<<<<< >>>>>

The following morning, Scaroon left Francesca so she could go to the shop and he went back to his gun club. Francesca was becoming very close with him and felt herself falling deeper in love and felt sorry to hear about his brother, but he had said nothing about the rebels, if he had anything to do with them, he was saying nothing so far.

'Good morning, Francesca, did your evening go well with Scaroon last night?' Kaleena asked.

Francesca smiled at Kaleena, but Kaleena saw something in her expression that said she had more to tell her. 'Yes, everything went well last night, but Scaroon told me why he had come to this area. It seems that someone around here, murdered his brother and he's come to find whoever it is and kill them for it. He didn't say anything about the rebels though, at least, not yet,' she said to Kaleena.

Kaleena looked at her with a serious expression, 'In that case, Francesca, he might be organising the gun club to gather rebels to satisfy his own revenge and the rebels are just part of his plan. You'll have to try and find out what he thinks about the Sky Gods and their ideas to build a city with our people.'

Francesca nodded to her, 'Yes, Kaleena, but I hope he doesn't get himself killed, I am beginning to like him a lot, needless to say, he stayed again last night.'

Kaleena smiled at her, 'I can see you have fell for him, Francesca, so be very careful, things could still go horribly wrong for both of you.'

'Yes, Kaleena, I know this, but I will be very careful, so don't worry about me, I will look-out for any signs of danger and keep away from it if it looks unsafe.'

'Very well, I saw Roella last night and told her about what happened with the man who attacked you, she will let Norak know and keep him up to date with what is happening. Are you seeing Scaroon again tonight?' Kaleena asked tentatively.

'Yes, but he said he would be around later as he had some business to attend to, but didn't say what it was and I didn't push the point, just in case it made him suspicious, but it's possible that he is meeting with the rebels, if he is, connected with them.'

'Well, done, Francesca, that was very wise, if he is connected to the rebels, he will hopefully choose his time to tell you, if he wishes too. But you could bring into the conversation about the Sky Gods and the new city, and see what he says about it, but do it casually so you don't throw any suspicion on yourself, the last thing we wish to happen is for you to get hurt or worse.'

'I understand, Kaleena, we'll have to wait and see how things plan out, but I am becoming very close to him and he might tell me in confidence once he has gained my complete trust.'

'We shall see, we shall see,' Kaleena said with other thoughts in her mind.

Kaleena was in the tavern waiting for Roella to join her, the tavern was full and several stories were going round about the murder of the man that tried to proposition Francesca, it seems that no one saw anything and his murderer was a complete mystery. Kaleena was pleased for that and knew that Scaroon had got away without being seen with Francesca on the night of the murder.

As Roella walked into the tavern, Kaleena waved her over to where she was sitting. The bar maid brought them a tankard of ale each as usual and they began to chat. Roella began, 'I have told Norak about Francesca's relationship with Scaroon and he hopes she will be very careful. He doesn't want anything to happen to her.'

'I have had this conversation with her and she assures me that she is being very cautious about what she talks to Scaroon about. She is very smart and her skills at the unarmed fighting arts are getting very good, she is very capable now of looking after herself,' Kaleena told Roella.

'That's good, Kaleena, does she think that Scaroon is connected with the rebels?' she asked.

'I'm not sure, nor is she, but she has found out that Scaroon came to live around here to find the murderer of his brother, he is set for revenge and will not leave until he has found out who is responsible and has dealt with him or them accordingly.'

Roella looked at Kaleena with a blank look, 'I see, then it is possible that the Gun Club is a genuine setup, but I hope Francesca doesn't get mixed up with any murders, it would be bad for her and Scaroon,' Roella said with concern.

'I think Francesca will be careful, but she did say today that although she was seeing him again tonight, he was going round to her apartment later after he'd been to see about some business. Francesca thinks that he might be going to a meeting with the rebels, if that is the case, then he will be involved with them. Francesca said she is going to ask him how he feels about the Sky Gods helping with the new city that has been planned, but she will wait until the time is right. I think she will be very careful how she approaches the subject.'

'I hope so, Kaleena, she is a lovely girl and smart, I'm glad you have her working with you in the shop.'

'Yes, so am I, she is very good at her job and works very well with the customers. I think she is going to be with me for some time, a long time I hope.'

Kaleena chatted with Roella for some time and left to go home. They hoped that Francesca would be careful and bring them more news of the situation with Scaroon and his possible connection to the rebels.

<<<<< >>>>>

As usual, Francesca was early at the shop the following day and full of the joys of life. She came in with a spring her feet and smiling happily, Kaleena noticed that she seemed extra happy and asked, 'I take it you had a good night last night?'

Francesca gave Kaleena a big smile and answered, 'Yes, Kaleena, Scaroon really excelled himself last night and made love to me like he'd never done before, he was incredible.'

Kaleena smiled at her almost chuckling at her, 'I'll ask no more about that side of your relationship, that's your affair, but I'm glad he is making you feel happy. Did he say anything about his meeting that he'd been to before coming to you?'

'Well, I asked him if his meeting went well, and he said it was a very successful and productive night, but he didn't go into detail and I'm still not sure if he is involved with the rebels.'

'Did you say anything to him about the Sky Gods and the new city?' Kaleena asked hoping she would have news for her.

'I didn't get around to it, he was more interested in us making love, so I didn't really get chance to ask him anything about them, but give me time and I will do, it has to be timed just right.'

'I agree, Francesca, but let me know what he says after you have asked him.'

'Don't worry, Kaleena, you'll be the first to know. I might get a chance tonight, I think he is going to be coming round most evenings now to stay, and I'm not complaining.'

Kaeelna just grinned at her and asked her no more concerning Scaroon. She knew that Francesca would tell her as soon as she knew anything concerning the rebels.

Chapter Seven

Shnark and his rebels go to Annarki:

Shnark, Jarako and Sheraba were sitting in a large round room with their other friends from Greylon and being taken to Annarki to begin their work of creating the new weapons and Tachyon drive engines. They were pleased that Barook had accepted their betrayal to the Greylons, but knew they dare not make any mistakes or cause the Annarki to think otherwise, or they would be killed.

Shnark looked at Jarako and Sheraba, 'Well, we have at last convinced the Annarki that we genuinely want to help them; I hope we can build and teach the Annarki scientist how to make the weapons and tachyon drives. I would expect the new weapons to be built first, they are of uttermost importance to the Annarki, I feel that the Greylon leaders are planning an attack on Annarki and hope to win and take over their planet, so we must get the weapons made and installed as quickly as possible.'

Jarak looked at Shnark with concern, 'I just hope the people from our planet give us time to build the weapons before they attack, or the Annarki could be in trouble.'

'Yes, that is true; we must push the production through as quickly as we can.'

Suddenly, the automatic doors to the round room opened and Barook came in and walked over to a podium that looked down to where the Greylons were sitting. He looked particularly at Shnark, Jarako and Sheraba and said, 'We have just learned that a few of the Greylon ships have left your planet, and are heading towards the fourth planet. Our ships are ready to defend it, but I hope that the Greylon ships haven't been fitted with the new weapons, or our defending ships could be in great danger,' he told them.

Jarako smiled at him and bravely said, 'I wouldn't worry too much about that, Barook, before we left, we rendered the components to the new weapons, that they had, unfit for their version of the weapon. They will be able to build them, but because of our sabotaging the components, when they try to use them, they will explode and destroy the ships they are fitted into.'

Barook looked at Jarako with intrigue, 'Jarako, are you saying that your people will not be able to use the weapons they build?'

'Yes, Barook, when they find out what's happened, they will have to begin production all over again and that will take time. By then, we shall have the weapons built for you and installed into your ships. You will be able to attack Greylon and defeat it if you do it immediately we have fitted the weapons into your ships.'

'That is very good news, Jarako, I commend your insight to our situation. We will be able to destroy the ships heading for Thaldernian without any problems.

We are now approaching Annarki and you will be well cared for and given all you need to build the new weapons and then the new tachyon drives.'

Sheraba, added, 'Barook, you do realise that the Tachyon drives are for travelling to the stars, they are too powerful to travel in between the planets,' she told him.

Barook looked at her, 'Yes, we had realised that, but it will make our space research of other worlds much more effective, but the weapons are priority as soon as we get to Annarki.'

Jarako nodded and looked at Barook, 'Fear not, Barook, we shall get to work on them as soon as we get to your planet. We are as keen to get them made as you are and know how important it is knowing what will happen to the Greylon ships when they try to use their new weapon against you.'

Barook smiled at Jarako, which was a rare thing for Barook to do, 'We will look forward to destroying all your war machines and make the Greylon's aware of who will be the most powerful race. Your planet will be taken over by our people and never be a threat to Thaldernian again,' he said and left them to talk amongst themselves until they reached Annarki.

<<<<< >>>>>

Shnark, Jaracko and Sheraba being followed by the other Greylon rebels were led into living quarters where they would be staying whilst on Annarki. Each of the

Greylons had an apartment and found them to be very comfortable with everything they needed. They had been told that they would be taken to the workshops to begin their weapon production later that day when they had settled in and had rested for a while.

Several hours later after they had rested and felt refreshed, they were taken to the large workshop where all the machinery was that they needed to produce the new weapons for the Annarki war ships. Shnark, Jarako and Sheraba organised their men and the Annarki scientist and Jarako began to explain how the components to the weapons were made and a set of the plans that Sheraba and Jarako had drawn were projected onto a large screen that showed all the components and explained how they were made and worked.

The head Annarki scientist was called Bolon and he worked with Jarako and Sheraba and learned how the components were to be made. The production began immediately and all the Greylon rebels were shown what to do so they could work alongside the Annarki engineers and scientists.

Ten Annarki war ships, including Ashtuk's had been informed about the Greylon war ships and what would happen when they tried to fire their new weapons at them. The Annarki army, on their separate ships, were prepared to fire on the Greylon ships and destroy them.

Ashtuk was in command as they approached the Greylon ships and waited to see what would happen when the Greylon ships were destroyed by the faulty weapons.

The overall Greylon ship commander, was Zemor and he stood on the control deck of the leading war ship and felt confident that they were about to destroy the Annarki patrol ships. He was in communication with the other four ships and gave the order for the new weapons to be aimed at the Annarki craft.

Ashtuk watched as the Greylon ships came into range to fire at them and waited to see what happened. Ashtuk was also in communication with all of his patrol ships that were equipped with the best weapons they had until the new ones had been fitted.

Zemor smiled as he looked at the Annarki ships on his forward monitor, he spoke into his console and said, 'Get ready to destroy the first five Annarki ships, on my command – now!'

Ashtuk and the other Annarki ship commanders watched as the five Greylon ships exploded into thousands of pieces.'

Everyone from all ten Annarki ships cheered loudly as they saw the Greylon ships explode. They never had to fire one weapon, Shnark and his scientist had done their jobs well as the Greylon ships were destroyed as they had told Barook they would be.

Ashtuk immediately contacted Barook on his forward monitor. Moments later, Barook appeared on the screen, 'Barook, the five Greylon ships exploded as Jarako predicted when they tried to fire at us, we can only hope now that Jarako and his teams on Annarki can get the new working weapons installed onto our ships before the Greylons can reproduce more of the weapons that will work.'

'That is good news, Ashtuk,' Barook said to him, 'I will inform Jarako and the others that what they said would happen to the Greylon ships, has happened. I am now eager to get our ships equipped with the new weapons; we will then destroy the Greylon forces once and for all.'

'That will be a day to look forward to, My Lord Barook, we shall be victorious and no more trouble from the Greylons, ever again.'

Barook nodded to Ashtuk and the screen went black. Ashtuk grinned to himself, and felt very happy at the outcome and couldn't wait to lead the attack on the Greylon Planet.

Barook walked into the large workshop where Jarako and all his men were working on the production of the new weapons. Shnark and Jarako were talking together when Barook walked up to them, 'I have good news, Shnark and for you Jarako, I have just received word from Ashtuk, the five Greylon ships with the faulty weapons were destroyed as they tried to fire on the

Annarki patrol ships. It is even more urgent to get the new weapons installed into our war ships, we want to attack the Greylon's planet and defeat them before they can re-make new working weapons,' he said to them.

Shnark and Jarako grinned at Barook, 'We are working well, My Lord Barook, they shall be finished in two days, I can assure you it will take the Greylons much longer to get the operational weapons built. You will soon be able to attack Greylon and destroy their forces and warships,' Jarako told him.

Barook slapped Jarako and Shnark on their shoulders as a well-done gesture and left them feeling very happy at the progress of the new weapons.

Shnark looked at Jarako and said, 'I think that Barook is happy with our results and the destruction of the Greylon ships, we need to make good progress and finish the new weapons. I will be sorry to see the Greylon forces destroyed, but we will have a better life from now on.

'Yes, Shnark, that is true, it means a new life for those with us and we can make much progress with the Annarki people,' Jaracko said.

<<<<< >>>>>

Snark, Jaracko and the rest of the teams together with the trained Annarki scientists and engineers, worked hard over the next two days and were ready to install the completed weapons into all the Annarki ships.

Barook came to see them and went to Shnark and Jaracko, 'I have received word that the weapons are ready to be installed into our ships.'

'Yes, My Lord Barook, we can begin to install them straight away, we have already begun to transport them to the individual ships,' Shnark told him.

'Well done, inform me as soon as the ships are fitted and ready to fly, we can't waste any time in attacking the Greylons. Their remaining ships will be defenceless against our updated weapons, thanks to you and you men, I will wait with eagerness for the report,' Barook said and left them to continue with the new weapon installations.

Two days later, the new weapons were installed into the Annarki war ships and the Annarki crews were ready to attack Greylon and destroy all their warships so the Annarki could take over their planet. Barook knew they would meet Greylon ships on their way to Greylon, but were confident that they would defeat them and go on to take-over the planet.

Chapter Nine

The Rebels take the Annarki ship:

The rebels had heard from their top leader that the Annarki ambassador was coming to visit Norak to discuss the building of the new city. What they were not expecting was the ambush that had been organised by the rebels to take over their ship. At the meeting of the rebels a few days before, Vertol had been assigned as the leader for the attack, it was decided that Scaroon should be kept from it and keep the front up and the running at the Gun Club to keep away any suspicion of the rebel forces meeting there.

They watched in hiding as the Annarki ship began to land. The plan was to let the ambassador leave and go to see Norak and then attack with the minimum crew and guards left behind when Vegor the ambassador was out of the way with his councillors. They were going to kill the two guards outside the ship with crossbows to make sure no one heard them and wouldn't attract attention from anyone who might be near to them. The Annarki ship landed in a piece of spare ground by the pavilion where Norak lived and met with his councillors. Norak was there to meet them with Voix and two other councillors.

'Greetings, Vegor, it is good to meet with you again, we have much to discuss, come, we have refreshments prepared for you after your long spaceflight.'

'Thank you, Norak, I think we shall make good progress today. Our people are looking forward to bringing our machinery to begin the groundwork's of the city,' Vegor said with a wide smile.

They all walked towards the pavilion entrance and disappeared into the building, leaving the two guards standing either side of the ramp that led into the spaceship.

Vertol gave a nod to the two men holding the crossbows, each stood up and aimed their bolts at the guards heart area and fired. Their aim was good and the two guards dropped to the floor with a crossbow bolt through their heart and died instantly.

Vertol and the others hurried to the spacecraft and dragged the two guards away behind a wall so no one would see them. Now all armed with firearms, they rushed into the ship and to the control room and killed anyone who got in their way who wasn't connected to the flight control crew.

They rushed into the control room bearing and pointing their guns at the flight controllers who flew the ship. They all stood there with their hands in the air and afraid they were all going to die.

Vertol spoke to them, 'If you don't want to die, you will do as I ask, you are to take off and plot a course to Greylon. Do it now or else suffer as your other crew has,' he said in a very stern and loud voice.

'One of the flight crew said, 'If we go towards Greylon, we shall be destroyed by the Greylon scout ships. We will be outnumbered and won't stand a chance,' he said.

Vertol looked at him again, 'Do as I say, we will take our chances, when we contact the Graylons, they will be told we are rebels and wish to join them and have information for them that they need to takeover Thaldernian.'

The flight commander turned to the controls and gave the order to do as Vertol had told them. The ship slowly lifted vertically and then headed for the sky and into outer-space.

When they got to cloud level, Vertol said, 'Go to the South Pole and set your course from there to Greylon, that way, your scout ships will not see our escape until it's too late, or not even see us at all,' he said.

The flight commander and crew did as he had told them and soon they were approaching the south pole of the planet. They set course for Greylon and sped off as fast as the ship would go, which was about twenty-five percent of light speed. They were soon approaching Greylon and slowed down ready to contact the Greylon patrol ships.

It wasn't long before they got a communication from the leading patrol craft of the Greylons. 'Annarki ship, why do you come here alone, we are ready to destroy your ship, state your business or we will fire on you,' the captain of the Greylon ship commanded.

Vertol stepped forward and the Greylon captain realised that this man was a Neanderthal, 'I am Vertol, a Neanderthal rebel who does not like the Annarki and what they plan to do. I have information to give to your leader about the Annarki plans to build cities on our planet, of which we do not agree with. We wish to join forces with you.'

'I am, Zernon, leading commander of the Greylon space force, how do we know you are not trying to get to our planet to cause trouble?' he asked.

Vertol looked sternly at Zernon, 'We have killed several Annarki crew to take this ship, if you wish to come aboard us and see, then do so. We want to create an alliance with you. We wish a meeting with Sholok,' he insisted.

Zernon looked at Vertol in his eyes as though reading his mind, as in truth, he was doing just that, Greylon's had telepathic abilities. Zernon nodded to Vegor after reading his thoughts, 'Very well, you will follow us in your ship, but do not make any false moves or we will destroy you immediately.'

Vertol smiled, 'We will do as you say, please take us to your planet so we can see Sholok,' he said.

The Greylon ship began to move towards the planet of Greylon and the Annarki ship followed.

Scaroon came into Francesca's apartment carrying a bag of food, he had brought it to compensate what they had used whilst he had been going to Francesca's apartment.

Francesca looked at him holding the bag in his hands, 'What have you got there, Scaroon, whatever it is, you have a lot of it,' she said with a warm voice.

Scaroon smiled at her, 'I have bought some food to replace what we have used whilst I have been coming here in the evenings, I thought it only right to put something back into your larder,' he answered her as he placed it on her table.

Francesca went to him and hugged him, and kissed him passionately. 'You didn't have to bring me any food. I can afford to feed you and enjoy doing so, but thank you anyway for your thoughts of my larder,' she said and added, 'You are a little late tonight to your usual time, have you had extra work at the Gun Club?' she asked.

Scaroon smiled at her as he held her to him, 'Nothing you need worry about, I just had a little business to deal with.'

Francesca smiled at him and said, 'Have you heard, there has been an Annarki ship stolen today, it was the ship that apparently brought the Annarki

Ambassador to see Norak, I'm guessing that they were going to discuss the new city they are going to build. Two guards were killed and a second ship had to come to take the Ambassador back again, it could mean something serious,' she said wondering what Scaroon's reaction would be.

Scaroon let her go and said, 'Yes, I have heard, it seems that some people don't want interference from the Annarki Sky Gods and that they should leave our planet alone,' he said in a voice that sounded not to be in agreement with what the Annarki wanted to do on Thaldernian.

Francesca smiled gently at him and said, 'Am I to take it that you don't want any interference from the Annarki Sky Gods?' she asked tentatively.

Scaroon looked at her with a blank look and she wondered if she had said something, she should not have. 'Francesca, I am a Neanderthal in and out and don't see the Annarki as Sky Gods as many do, I think they should leave our planet alone and respect what we want to do with it. I know they protect it from the Greylon's, but as far as I'm concerned, that's where they should stay and do, and leave the people of our planet to get on with our lives.'

'Well, I agree with you in letting them leave us alone, but we all know that the Greylon's want to destroy our planet after they have taken all precious metals and minerals from it, and kill all the

Neanderthals, so I'm thankful for the Annarki protecting us with their spacecraft.'

Scaroon smiled at her and asked, 'Francesca, it is believed by some of the Neanderthals that the Annarki only want us as hired slaves to do all their hard work for them and then leave us to struggle without them. These people don't want them on our world.'

Francesca realised that Scaroon was against the Annarki and wanted to change the ugly mood that was building, 'Well, Scaroon, on a lighter note, I have been shopping today and bought you a present.'

She turned and went to a cupboard and took out a parcel and gave it to him. 'What have you bought me, I wasn't expecting you buying me things,' he said with a smile.

Francesca was relieved at his warm smile and words, 'Well, Scaroon, you have made me so happy since we got together, I wanted to say a small thank you, so open your present and see what you think,' she said to him wanting him to do it there and then.

Scaroon smiled and opened the wrapping and found a brand new leather belt with beautiful carvings on it of different kinds of weapons. He gave Francesca a big hug and a kiss, 'It's beautiful, I shall always treasure it,' he looked at her deeply and added, 'you do know I have fallen in love with you don't you?' he said.

She kissed him back and said, 'I too have fallen in love with you. I want you, Scaroon, right now,' she said holding his hand and taking him to where her bed was. For the rest of the evening and night, they were in the throes of love making and enjoying each other's bodies.

<<<<< >>>>>

The following morning as Francesca walked into Kaleena's shop, the first thing Kaleena said to her was, 'Have you heard about the stolen Annarki spaceship?

Francesca nodded to her, 'Yes, I have and I know something else too. Scaroon doesn't agree with the Annarki Sky Gods building the new city or helping our people in any way, he believes we should be left alone. I now think he has some connection to the rebels. He told me last night that he feels the Annarki just want us Neanderthals as slaves to help build their city and then abandon us. '

Kaleena looked at her with a concerned look, 'Does he suspect anything about you and me?'

'No, Kaleena, he freely told me his thoughts about the Annarki, he has said that he knows that there are other people who think the same as he does, but he didn't say any more. I changed the subject as the atmosphere became tense, but I'm sure he doesn't know anything about us and Norak.'

'That's good, keep me updated so I can pass any useful information to Roella so she can tell Norak.'

'Will do, Kaleena, I'm in fear for Scaroon though, we both declared our love for each other last night and I don't want anything to happen to him,' Francesca said.

'I see, in that case, let's hope we can keep him from being involved. If you find he is, it means, he could be connected to the Annarki spacecraft being stolen and the two Annarki soldiers being killed. That could make things serious for him.'

Francesca looked at Kaleena with a sad expression, 'I will find out more over the next few days, we have agreed for him to live with me at my apartment and maybe become mated officially at some point.'

'We shall have to see how things work out,' Kalenna said in a hopeful voice.

Later that day, Scaroon came into the Gun Shop to see Kaleena and Francesca, 'Hello, Scaroon,' Kaleena greeted him, 'is this a social call or is it business?' she asked with a warm smile.

He chuckled at Kaleena's question, 'Well, it's a bit of both actually, firstly I wish to order twenty more Guns the same as I had before, ten rifles and ten hand guns, I also want ten more crossbows and ten Bows, complete with arrows and crossbow bolts.'

Kaleena and Francesca smiled at him, 'My word, Scaroon, business is getting good for you it seems,' Kaleena said.

'Yes, my club is getting very popular, I am really pleased about it, I'm also pleased that Francesca and I have got together, I take it she has told you we are seeing each other,' he said with enthusiasm in his voice.

Kaleena laughed at him, 'Oh yes, Scaroon, since you two have started seeing each other, she floats around this shop as if in another world,' she said looking across to Francesca and smiling at her.

They all laughed and Francesca blushed a little, Scaroon walked over to the counter where Francesca was standing, 'Do I have that much impact on you, Francesca?' he asked her with a wide grin.

Francesca didn't quite know what to say, she grinned back at him and answered, 'Let's just say that I'm happier now than I've been for a long time, and it's all because of you,' she said smiling at him.

Scaroon put his hand across the counter and squeezed Francesca's hand, 'My life has become meaningful too, I'll see you later, bye for now,' he said and left the shop.

Kaleena looked at Francesca and smiled, 'You make a good couple, I think that you're head over heels with each other, and hope Scaroon doesn't get in too deep with the rebels, he is a nice man with a rough exterior.'

'Yes, Kaleena, I agree, I want him to keep away from the rebels if he is connected with them, I hope he finds the true murderer of his brother and deals with him and then leave the rebels to their own devices.'

'We can only hope, Francesca, meanwhile, I'll put the order in for Scaroons weapons to our suppliers, his Gun Club has certainly boosted our sales,' she said with a smile.

Scaroon walked into Francesca's apartment and gave her a big hug and a kiss, 'So how has your day been, Francesca?' he asked.

'Very busy at the shop, it's been a good day, and thank you for calling in, I think Kaleena is very happy for us,' she told him, 'how as your day been?'

'It's been good, the club's membership is growing and I think it will become the biggest club of its kind in these parts.'

'That's good,' Francesca answered him, but sensed a little tension within his words. 'Scaroon, you seem to be a little tense, is there something wrong that you're not telling me?' she asked with a loving voice.

Scaroon looked at her with compassion, 'I have a problem with one of my men, I think that he is the one who killed my brother and I'm not sure what to do about him. My instincts tell me to do away with him and leave the area, but things have become awkward now I have the club and my love for you. I don't want to lose either of you.'

Francesca hugged him and said, 'You can always let the past go and concentrate on the present, but I can understand how you feel, you are going to have to come to terms with it, I don't want to lose you either, if you go away, I want to go with you, but your club is doing so well. I hope you make the right choice in all this confusion you have.'

Scaroon looked her straight in her eyes and then kissed her passionately. He pulled back and said, 'You are right, I need to decide, but it is going to be a hard choice to make, If I am right and it is the man I suspect that killed my brother, I am going to want to kill him, but now we are so close, I don't want anything to come between us.'

'I know, Scaroon, but justice will have its way in the end, his evil killing of your brother will come back to him without any action from you, trust me, his actions will be paid back to him in another way,' she said to him and hoping he would believe her and accept what she'd said.

'We shall have to wait and see, I still need to know for sure if the one I think it is, is the right man, I'll then decide after I know.'

'I'm sure you will make the right decision, Scaroon, you know what's at stake,' Francesca assured him.

Chapter Ten

Defeat of the Greylons:

Ashtuk's ten ships had been recalled back to Annarki to have the new weapons installed and were replaced by ten more that had the weapons in operational readiness. When Astuk's ships had been fitted with the weapons, they joined all the other warships in orbit around Thaldennian and were ready to attack Greylon.

Barook had learned about the Annarki ship that had been hi-jacked, and was furious and was now hell bent on revenge against the Greylons.

Barook made Ashtuk the overall commander of the attacking fleet that numbered fifty war ships in all. They were all poised and waiting for Barook to join Ashtuk on his ship. Barook wanted to be there as the battle commenced. Barook's personal craft docked on to Ashtuk's and Barook quickly made his way to the control room.

'Welcome aboard My Lord Barook, we are ready to move to Greylon and attack it, but we know there will be some resistance and that their ships will not have the new weapons yet. They will not know that we have them yet either, until we fire on them.'

'Very good, Commander Ashtuk, give the order to begin the journey towards Greylon, this is going to be a great day in our history. We have been at war for eight years with the Greylon's, now we are going to defeat them once and for all,' Barook said, then Added, 'I take it you have heard about what happened with the Annarki ship on Thaldernian, the Greylons will pay dearly for their actions.'

'Yes, My Lord Barook, I have heard, as you say, the Greylons will pay for their actions and the Neanderthal rebels too.' Ashtuk gave the command to all the other warships and they began to move towards Greylon for the onslaught.

'How many Greylon ships are we to expect, My Lord Barook, did you ask Shnark and his men if they knew how many ships they had?'

'Yes I did, it seems they have about sixty war crafts, but won't have the new weapons. This means we shall be within attacking range with the new weapons before the Greylon's will be in range with their lesser powerful weapons, we should be able to destroy a large number of their ships before they can aim at us and the rebel ship too, that is one of ours.'

'Very well, My Lord, as soon as we are in range, we will commence firing, we should destroy most of their ships before they attack ours, if not all.'

<<<<< >>>>>

As the Annarki approached Greylon, they saw a host of Greylon ships coming to meet them. The Greylon's had been informed by their scout ships about the Annarki attack force. Before the Annarki ships were in range to use their new weapons, the Greylon's opened fire, but were too far away to make any difference to the Annarki craft.

Barook and Ashtuk just laughed at their puny attempts to shoot at them. The Annarki ships were able to destroy the Greylon weapons heading for their ships before they did any damage to them.

Soon, the Annarki were in range to use their new weapons and they opened fire on the Greylons. It was almost a massacre as each one of the Greylon ships was destroyed, including the Annarki ship that was hijacked and with all the rebels on it, was also blasted by the Annarki ships' new weapons.

There were only three Greylon ships left when Ashtuk got a communication from one of them. The commander of the third Greylon ship showed himself on the forward monitor of Ashtuk's craft, 'We surrender to your powers, please don't destroy our last three ships,' he almost pleaded.

Barook came into view on the monitor and looked at the Greylon Commander as he begged them not to destroy them, 'Why should we spare you, you have been the scourge of our planet and now we have superior weapons and could destroy your last three ships and your planet if we so chose to do so.'

'Please, Lord Barook, we surrender in complete humility, we will join you and allow your soldiers to board our ships and take them over, we are begging for our lives.'

Barook was pleased that they hadn't lost one ship, thanks to the new weapons and decided to do as the Greylon commander had asked.

Barook looked directly into the eyes of the Greylon Commander, 'Very well, we will do as you ask, all three of your puny ships will dock onto my ship and be prepared to become our prisoners. But any false move and you will be destroyed immediately, do you understand,' he growled at the Greylon Commander.

'I understand, Lord Barook, we will come to you and do as you say, I promise you that we will not betray our word.'

The Annarki war ships were much larger than the Greylons, and the Greylon ships could dock onto the Annarki ships without a problem, Barook now knew he had the Greylon at the Annarki's mercy.

Soon the Greylon's were docking onto Astuk's ship and the three commanders from them were brought to the Annarki's control room where Barook and Ashtuk were waiting for them. The three Greylon ships were taken over by the Annarki guards and the Greylon crews were taken to a secure place until it was decided what was going to happen to them.

Annarki Guards brought the three Greylon commanders into the control room, they were made to stand before Barook and were terrified of what was going to happen to them and almost trembled visibly.

Barook looked at them, 'If you want me to spare your lives, you will show me everywhere on your planet where your space craft are made and other areas where they operate from, we shall destroy them once and for all and your planet will be under our control. Your leader, Sholok will surrender to us and accept your planet's defeat and being taken over by my people. If this does not happen, we will terminate you and your crews and destroy Greylon's atmosphere completely and leave it desolate forever. Do you understand!' he said in a loud voice.

They Greylon Commanders nodded and agreed, 'We will do our part, Lord Barook, if you will spare our lives and our people on Greylon, but Sholok might resist with his personal guards and ship. He may try to escape the planet before you can capture him.

Barook was still looking directly at the three Greylon Commanders, 'If he escapes, we will find him and destroy his ship, we now have superior engines that will easily overtake his puny ship and he will be destroyed.'

The three Greylon's looked at Barook with fear and were not aware of the new tachyon engines that were now fitted to the Annarki ships.

Barook looked at the guards with the three Greylons, 'Take these Greylons back to their crews and put them in the secure area until I decide what to do with them.'

The guards did as Barook said and he watched as they left the control room of the Annarki leader's ship.

Sholok had received news that his fleet of warships had been destroyed and knew that he was now at the Annarki's mercy and wasn't about to stay around to face Barook. He knew Barook's reputation and his hate for the Greylons.

Sholok sent for his personal guards and waited to hear more from the loss of his war ships. He had two options and the thought of the Annarki taking over and his fate was too much to ask. His personal guards came to him. He stood before them and said, 'Well my trusted guards, you know by now what has happened, we will go to my personal ship and leave this planet and try and find another world to live on, but we don't know how long that will take.'

One of his guards asked, 'My Lord, Sholok, are we going to take our families with us?'

Sholok looked at him unsure; he knew they would have a better chance staying on Greylon, under Annarki rule, than taking their chances on his ship. He also knew that if the Annarki found them that they would destroy them, so he decided to leave his family and the guards families on Greylon to take their chances and have a better chance of surviving with the Annarki.

Sholok looked at his guard who had asked about their families, 'I know you have loved ones here on Greylon, but at this time, we cannot afford to take them with us. If the Annarki get to know where we are, they will surely come after us and destroy us, that would mean our families as well, they don't have mercy on anyone trying to escape, especially me, Barook hates me as much as I hate him, my fate is sealed if he finds me. We will go now to my personal ship and hope we can keep out of the way of the Annarki.'

Sholok and his guards headed for Sholok's ship and prepared to leave Greylon. All the guards with families and Sholok himself, made their good byes quickly and set off away from Greylon before the Annarki ship would be close enough to follow them and catch them up, not knowing about the new tachyon engines the Annarki now had.

Sholok escaped and was soon heading for another planetary system. The Annarki were now heading towards the Greylon planet to destroy all their bases and plants where they had built the Greylon ships and other related aspects of the Greylon fleet.

The three Greylon Commanders had been brought back to the control room on Ashtuks ship to help direct the Annarki fleet to the appropriate areas on Greylon they were going to destroy. Although Barook was a hard man, he wasn't evil, and was going to give the workers of the Greylons time to move from the factories and workshops before destroying them.

The Greylon Commanders gave information as to where the workshops and factories were on their planet. They were scattered about in different isolated parts, and Barook instructed his ships to follow the directions from the Greylon commanders and find them. They were instructed that all workers in these areas were to be evacuated before the units were blasted and destroyed.

Over the next few hours, the appropriate areas were evacuated and the industrial units where the Greylon ships had been made were destroyed and raised to the ground.

Barook now moved to the planet with the rest of his war fleet, and headed for their main cities and sent word that all Greylons were to gather in places where they could hear Braook's transmissions to them all.

Transmissions were sent back to Annarki and Snark, Jarako and Sheraba were told about the takeover of the Greylon planet. Everyone was happy to hear the news and were not surprised to hear that Sholok had escaped with his faithful crew and guards. Spirits were high and celebrations were promised back on Annarki to remember the takeover of the Greylon planet. Eight years of war had come to an end, and no more would the Annarki have to patrol the planet of the Neanderthals of Thaldernian.

A transmission was also sent to Norak to tell him the good news about the Greylon surrender to the

Annarki. Norak didn't waste any time letting Roella know so she could tell Kaleena and Francesca.

Word soon got around Thaldernian and the whole planet were having their own celebrations in every city and town. The only ones who were not happy were the rebels and were already planning disruptions to the Annarki building of any cities that were planned on Thaldernian.

Chapter Eleven

New Plans:

Barook had arranged to go to the Greylon head city that was where Sholok had ruled from and make his transmission to all the people from there. As he was walking up the long stairs to the main building, there was a shot from the side of a row of buildings. The laser fire missed Barook by inches and he ducked down behind his personal guards. The man who shot at him was seen escaping and was chased by the Annarki soldiers. The man was soon apprehended and brought to the building where Barook was going to make his speech from, Barook was not pleased at the attempt on his life.

The man it turns out was the son of one of the personal guards to Sholok who had gone off with him when they escaped. He was angry and wanted to take his revenge for his father having to leave with Sholok. His name was Lurak, and missed his father very much and *was* going to join the Greylon forces in a year's time.

Barook decided to give his speech first before dealing with Lurak and wanted him to sit with fear in a cell before meeting Barook. Barook made his way to the transmission room where his message would go out to the Greylon people.

He stood before the screen that looked out over the city he was in with other smaller screens showing other parts of the planet and gatherings.

He began, 'People of Greylon, you all know who I am, and you also know I am not a patient man, but contrary to popular belief, I do have a sense of compassion. It is possible that some of you have not agreed with what your leaders were doing in space, regarding Thaldernian, the Neanderthal Planet. They had planned to destroy all the people and spare none. They just wanted to plunder, kill and rape the land for its resources then leave the planet desolate;' he paused for a few moments to let his words sink into the people's minds. He then carried on, 'However, I am not an evil mercenary like your leaders were, they are cowards and have escaped unable to face their sentences of the sheer wanting of destruction to Thaldernian and its people. Your planet can carry on as it has always done; the only difference is that there will be no Greylon spaceships or anyone to cause war with our home planet. We will work with you and create a council of leaders that will have Greylon members and Annarki members so things can be agreed fairly. I hope this meets with your approval. I assure you all that your lives will be better under our rule than with Sholok.'

He watched the reaction of the people on the monitors in the transmission room, most of the people seemed to be happy with the ideas put to them. He hoped that it would pacify all the Greylons.

'However,' he continued, 'we shall not tolerate any rebellion. Anyone who decides they want to rebel and cause any disruption in any way will be arrested and then sent to the Annarki prison moon, where they will never leave again and it is inescapable.'

The reaction was a mixed one, but now they knew the consequences of rebellion, and were strongly advised to work with the Annarkians.

Barook turned from the transmission screen and had said all he was going to do for the moment; he was satisfied with the Greylons reactions to his words. He was now prepared to meet Lurack who took a shot at him before entering the building. He looked at one of his guards and instructed him to bring the boy before him; he was only about eighteen years old.

A short time later, Lurack was brought before Barook. As he walked into the room where Barook was waiting for him, he was marched between two large Annarkian guards who stood much taller than he was and broader and sporting laser rifles.

He was looking down at the ground and now wishing he hadn't tried to kill Barook. Barook was sitting in a large chair and was at the same eye-level with Lurak. Barook looked at him and said, 'I understand your name is, Lurak, I would appreciate it if you looked at me and not at the floor, you show bad manners boy by doing that, and don't do your parents any justice by doing so.'

Lurak slowly lifted his head and looked at Barook with an unfriendly expression, 'What have you to say for yourself, Lurak?' Barook asked him.

Lurak had no hesitation in saying, 'Because of you, my father has been forced by Sholok to leave this planet and he will possibly never return again. I wanted to kill you so much, but I failed.'

Barook almost smiled at his arrogance, 'Lurak, had you have killed me, you would now be on your way to our prison planet, and believe me, you would have hated yourself many times over for your actions should you have succeeded in killing me. However, you didn't succeed, and I can understand why you hate me so much, however, I can understand how you feel having lost your father and may not see him again. I am a hard man, but I am not heartless, I do have feelings and have a son about your age on Annarki, although some might debate I have compassion, I do and feel for your loss. I will give you several choices, you can continue to rebel, in which case you will certainly finish up on the prison moon, or you can work with our people, and ruling, and enjoy moderate freedom and do most of what you wish to do. If, and I say if, you work well and don't cause me any trouble, you might be considered to sit on the planet council and help make the decisions that affect everyone on Greaylon, this would be a great honour for you and your family. I will make you a promise, if we ever catch up with Sholok and his guards with him, I will only want to take Sholok and punish him appropriately, but all those with him I will spare and give them a chance to work with everyone else, that means, you will see your father again.'

Lurak, looked at him with a different expression and noted what Barook had just said about sparing Sholok's guards, one being his father. He said to Barook, 'If you hold your promise and save my Father, I will work with your people and cause you no problems, I certainly don't wish to go to your prison moon, I have heard about it and what it's like. I give you my promise and word to do my best if your promise is kept.'

Barook now gave one of his rare smiles and said, 'Lurak, you have impressed me, and believe me, that isn't easy, but I see greatness in you and one day your family will be proud of you if you do as you promise, I assure you that I will keep mine. If anything happens to your father, it will not be by my hand, and I will personally deal with anyone who harms him. I cannot be any fairer than that.'

Lurak smiled back at Barook and answered, 'In that case, Barook , we have a bargain and a covenant of trust between us, I will honour it with my heart and look forward again to seeing my Father, Curin.'

'Very good, Lurak, you may go back to your family and I will contact you as soon as I get word of your Father, but be patient, it may take some time for us to find Sholok and those with him.

Scaroon came into Francesca's apartment after a long day at the Gun Club and was obviously tired. He sat down in a large chair by the fire and almost fell to sleep. Francesca went to him, and gave him a welcoming-home kiss and sat on his lap.

'I take it you have had a tiring day at the Gun Club?' she asked him.

'He smiled up at her and pulled her to him and kissed her, 'Yes, you could say that, it is going very well and the regular members are coming nearly every day. It is growing.' He looked at her with love in his eyes, he had truly fallen in love with her in completeness and she was now his soul mate and lover. 'It is so nice be able to come home to such a beautiful woman who loves me and looks after me. I hope we never part, Francesca,' he said with a slight sadness in his tone.

Francesca noticed his underlying sadness, 'You say that, Scaroon with a little reserve, is there something wrong that you are not telling me?' she asked with concern.

He looked her in her beautiful dark eyes and said, 'Nothing to worry about, I'm just hoping that this planet keeps its independence from the Annarki, we don't need them here, we are fine as we are and I wouldn't welcome their change, but I know it's coming and it bothers me.'

Francesca looked at him lovingly, 'I don't know why you worry about them, Scaroon, they are coming to help make our lives better with their advanced ideas. Why does it bother you so?'

Scaroon looked at her and knew he should be angry with her, but he loved her so much he just couldn't find words of anger to use, he grinned and answered, 'Francesca, we shall just have to agree to differ on the subject of the Annarki, if they come, they come and there is nothing I can do about it. While I think about it, I will be late tomorrow night, I have to go to a meeting to discuss the possibility of setting up another gun club in Skinsville, we have got a lot of members coming from there and they have suggested I start another Gun Club there to save them coming all the way here to Norsville.'

Francesca smiled at him, 'Does that mean our shop can expect another large weapons order?' she asked.

Scaroon laughed at her, 'Maybe so, I'll let you know what happens tomorrow, but I want to hold off for a while if I can, I don't feel ready to expand just yet, but we will have to wait and see.'

Francesca leaned over and kissed him passionately, and then left him to rest whilst she finished making their evening meal of deer stew and dumplings. As she stirred the stew, she couldn't help thinking that the meeting that Scaroon had just told her about was in reality another meeting with the rebels. She would wait and see what he said when he came back from it the following night.

The following day, Scaroon met in secret with the main leader, who was disguised so as not to be recognised. Scaroon was curious as to why he wanted to see him.

They met in the busy market place behind one of the stalls where no one would question their presence.

The man came to Scaroon after he had got there, and immediately went to him and said, 'I have bad news, Scaroon, The Annarki space fleet have taken over the Greylon planet and the ship that was stolen has been destroyed by the Annarki. The rebels, who hijacked it, have been killed. This is not good. I also know that in a few days that the Annarki are going to begin bringing their land moving machines and begin making the ground ready for building their city. We must plan to destroy it when they have begun to lay the foundations. At your meeting tonight, you need to tell them what I have told you and watch the situation carefully. They plan to build their city about two miles away from our town,' the man told him.

'As you say, this is not good, I will pass on your news tonight and we will begin to plan the disruptions in any way we can. Keep me informed so I can make the required arrangements to attack the new building site.'

'I will, Scaroon, now go back to your Gun Club and make ready for tonight's meeting, I will be in touch,' the man said to him and left him whilst Scaroon walked the other way. Scaroon, was also disguised in old clothing and hood to partially cover his face.

All the rebels were gathered in the large barn behind Scaroon's Gun Club, where he stored spare weapons in large crates until they were needed. Scaroon went and stood on a pile of planks and looked over everyone who was waiting to hear what he had to say.

He began, 'Today I have been told that the space craft we hijacked has been destroyed by the Annarki and that they have conquered the Greylon planet and taken it over. Sholok has escaped into space somewhere, but I have no doubt that the Annarkians will follow them and try to find Sholok and his crew. I also know that the Annarkians are planning to bring their earth moving machinery in a few days, and are going to begin preparing the ground to build their new city. It will be about two miles south from here. We need to be ready to go and disrupt it with explosives and slow them down as much as possible.'

'Scaroon, where are we going to get explosives from, the Gun Shop doesn't deal in explosives, only weapons?' Zimack asked.

Scaroon nods to him and says, 'There must be somewhere where we can get explosives from, even if we have to go to one of the larger towns to get them,' he said.

One of the Rebels called, Garaman suggested, 'Scaroon, there is a stone quarry to the west of town, we could break in there and steel some from them. I know they use explosives, it's called Sycronite and a small amount can do a lot of damage, my brother works there and has told me about it and where they store it. It shouldn't be difficult to get our hands on some, but there are two security guards there every night, we might have to take care of them first,' he told Scaroon.

Scaroon nodded at Garaman, 'That is good, Garaman, will you take some men and break in there tonight and get as much Sycronite as you can.'

'Yes, Scaroon, but I thought you'd want to come, why don't you?' Garaman asked him.

Scaroon answered him quickly, 'Because I am well known for the Gun Club, if I am seen and recognised, our cover will be broken, and cause us much trouble. It's best if I keep out of sight so I can keep face with the public and organise the meetings and actions without anyone knowing I am leading you,' he said hoping that everyone would understand.

Most of the rebels accepted what he said, but there were one or two who were unsure, but said nothing at that time. The one that was more concerned about Scaroon was Miraka, he had never really liked Scaroon, but held his council until a better time.

Scaroon looked round at them and said, 'Right, if that's all to be said, we will disperse and meet at the end of the week in four days time. But I want you, Garaman, to get what sycronite you can and bring it here and store it behind the Gun Club and cover it up well to disguise it from anything around it, can you do that?' he asked.

Garaman nodded, 'Yes, Scaroon we can do that, I will call and see you at the Gun Club tomorrow and show you what we got and how it went.'

'Very good, I'll see you tomorrow then, now we can go home and I'll let you all know what we are to do next when we meet at the end of the week, by then, the Annarki will have begun to bring their land moving machines.'

Everyone dispersed and went back to their homes. Scaroon left after locking up and went to Francesca who was eagerly awaiting his return.

As he walked into her apartment, she came to him and hugged him and kissed him with a welcoming kiss, 'How did your meeting go, did you put them off starting another Gun Club for a while?' she asked, wondering what he would say.

Scaroon smiled at her and answered, 'Yes, I put them off for about six months and told them to wait and see how the club went here first and that it had just started to build up. They were happy with that,' he said lying through his teeth, but she accepted what he said to her.

'That's good, Scaroon, but it's good to hear that the Gun Club is becoming well known in other towns too,' she said.

'Yes, Francesca, it is, I have also heard that the Greylon planet has been defeated by the Annarki ships, that means that they will be coming soon to begin building their city here, I must confess, it doesn't please me.'

Francesca smiled at him not wanting him to get in a bad mood about the Annarki, she knew how he felt about them, 'Scaroon, how do you feel about going to the Grewlers Tavern tonight, I'm meeting Kaleena and her sister Roella there, you haven't met Roella yet have you?' she suggested to him.

'No, I haven't, I think that would be a good idea, we haven't been out together in the true sense, I would like that. Yes, we will go as soon as we have eaten.

Scaroon wasn't aware that it was Kaleena's and Roella's idea to bring Scaroon with her for a meeting, but just socially, not business. As they walked in, Kaleena and Roella were already there. They went over to the table where they were sitting and joined them.

Francesca introduced Scaroon to Roella, 'Roella, this Scaroon, my man, he was happy to join us tonight.'

Scaroon shook Roella's hand, 'Pleased to meet you, Roella, what do you do for a job?' he asked, but just casually.

'I work for the High Council, Norak in particularly.'

Scaroons eyebrows lifted at hearing this, 'It must be very interesting work doing what you do,' he said with a smile.

'It is, Scaroon, you get to know all that's happening and plans for the town.'

Scaroon smiled at her, 'You will know about my Gun Club then?' he asked her.

'Yes, I understand it's doing well, I wish you luck with it, I think it has caused great interest and Kaleena says her sales are doing well because of it.'

'They all laughed at Roella's comment.

Scaroon chuckled at her and said, 'Yes, I have bought quite a few things from her and it's because of Kaleena's weapon's shop that I met Francesca, I am so happy about that.'

Roella added, 'Yes, Scaroon, I understand so, I'm very happy for you both, I hope things go well for you.'

'Thank you, Roella, it's kind of you to say so,' Scaroon said with a smile.

Roella then said, 'Did you know about the Greylon planet being taken over by the Annarki, No more threats by them attacking Thaldernian again, we are free of them at last, and the Annarki are going to build a new city where some of us can all live and enjoy their advancements.' She said with enthusiasm.

Francesca looked at Scaroon as if to say, *Say nothing*.

Kaleena added, 'Yes, we have heard, it's all over town, it doesn't take long for that kind of news to get around. Norak made no secret of it; he must have told his councillors who in turn have told others.'

Roella was unaware of Scaroons thoughts on the Annarki, he had only told Francesca what he thought about them, but Roella asked him, 'Scaroon, don't you think it's good news to know the Greylon's have been defeated at last?' she asked him. Francesca held her breath almost and hoped that Scaroon wouldn't make an issue of it about what he really thought.

Scaroon smiled at Roella, 'Well, Roella, we will have to see how things work out with the Annarki, but I fear not everyone will like their being around us too much,' he said in a way as not to rouse any suspicion.

'That's true, Scaroon,' Kaleena added, 'I have had one or two people in the shop today who are not too keen on the Annarki, so as you say, we shall have to wait and see what happens in the days to come,' she said.

Francesca smiled at Scaroon as though saying thank you to him for not saying too much of what he really thought. He smiled back at her and gave a slight nod that only she would understand.

Chapter Twelve

Plans in Action:

Garaman and six others quietly approached the outer fence of the quarry and bent down by the fencing. Garaman took out his wire cutters and began to cut a hole in the wire big enough for them to get through and back out with the explosives. It was a dark night without any moon, and there was only one searchlight rotating from the top of the security guard's hut that lit up the site. They quietly crawled through the hole in the fence and headed for the shed where the explosives were stored.

Snike used his crowbar to force the lock to get into the shed and successfully prized it open. They went in with their flashlights and found three cases of Sycronite. They quietly lifted each box, and took them outside, but as the last man were coming out of the shed, he tripped over and the box he was carrying smashed open causing a loud crash. Within seconds, the two security guards came running out of their hut.

Garaman had a gun and shot at the two men before they could fire at them, they both hit the ground believed to be dead. As they carried the two remaining boxes towards the fence, one of the security guards was able to lift his hand and shot Snike in the back and killed him; the guard then rolled over and died from his wound.

Jerone was about to go back and get Snike, but Garaman said, 'Leave him, he's dead,' and Jerone turned and followed the other five men crawling through the hole in the fence. Jerone looked back once more and then followed the others and disappeared into the night.

They quickly headed back to the Gun club and hid the Sycronite behind the club as told to by Scaroon.

After hiding the Sycronite, they all dispersed and went home. They were sorry for their loss of Snike, but it couldn't be helped and they needed to get away as quick as possible and make their escape.

The following day, Garaman went to see Scaroon at the Gun club and told him about Snike and what had happened, Scaroon wasn't happy about what had taken place and the loss of Snike as he was a good man and well liked by the others.

'I haven't looked behind the Club yet, Garaman, did you hide the explosives well?' he asked him.

'Yes, Scaroon, it's safe and dry until we need to use it. We were able to get two full boxes with twenty sticks in each and plenty to do what we need it for; one stick alone will do much damage to the site. If we place them well, we shall cause the Annarki much disruption.'

'Very good, now we need to let the Annarki get so far before we strike with the explosives.'

'Yes, Scaroon, we hope it will hold them up for a good time, but they will carry on and re-do what we damage of their site.'

'That is so, Garaman, but they will know that there's some that don't agree with what they are doing. What we will do next after our first attack remains to be seen. Go now and act and do as you would normally do and don't attract any attention to yourself.'

'Very well, Scaroon, I'll see you in three days at the next meeting.'

Garaman left Scaroon and Scaroon carried on at the club as though nothing had happened, only the member rebels knew about what had occurred and who had been responsible for the break-in at the rock quarry.

At the end of the day, Scaroon went back home to Francesca as though it was a normal day and said nothing to her regarding the break-in at the quarry. As he walked in, Francesca greeted him with a warm smile and a welcoming kiss, 'Have you had a good day, Scaroon, it's been very busy at the shop,' she asked him.

He smiled casually at her and said, 'Yes, it been another good day and we have three more new members too, how has your day been?' he asked her in return of her question.

'Well, one of the customers told us that he had heard about a break-in at the local stone quarry, it seems that the two guards were killed and one of the rebels was killed also, but they escaped with two boxes of explosives. It's quite scary when you think about it, who knows what they are going to do with it.'

Scaroon looked at her with a serious expression, 'Let's not worry about it, Francesca, it doesn't concern us, that's what's important, what the rebels do they do and that's all I want to say about them.'

Francesca smiled at him and Scaroon went to sit down in his adopted seat by the fire. He had become to be very comfortable with her and had settled in very nicely. He hoped it would always be the same, but deep down considered his involvement with the rebels. He hadn't anticipated the danger of killing people that had nothing to do with him, he only came to kill the man who killed his brother, but he'd found himself leading the rebels and wasn't sure if he wanted to continue, he was in deeper that he had intended. He pondered on his situation and waited for Francesca to make the evening meal, of whatever it was.

As he sat thinking, Francesca was watching him from her kitchen and realised he was in deep thought, in the back of her mind was the break-in of the quarry and hoped he had nothing to do with it, even though he had been with her, Kaleena and Roella the night before, when the robbery had taken place.

She went across to him and sat on his knee, which distracted his mood, she was wearing a low cut top that showed off her cleavage very well and knew he would be looking at her. 'What is it Scaroon, you look troubled?'

He watched her and smiled, and then looked at her breasts moving up and down as she was breathing. 'Francesca, you are a very sexy lady, and I look forward to making love to you tonight, I think of you many times a day and hope one day we won't have to think about the Annarki and the Greylons and such things, I want us to be with each other and have no interruptions.'

Francesca grinned at him, 'You are changing the subject, Scaroon, I have come to know when something is bothering you, do you want to talk about it?' she asked with love in her voice.

He smiled back her warmly and said, 'I'm just thinking about this Annarki thing and them becoming part of our society, I am not looking forward to them wandering around in our town or us becoming part of *their* society, it's wrong!'

'Well, Scaroon, you might change your mind when you see the advantages of their technology; they are going to make some amazing changes that we can all enjoy.'

'I still don't like the idea, they are ugly creatures compared to us and I don't trust them, they are also bigger and stronger than our people and that makes for disharmony as some will feel very uncomfortable with it.'

Francesca gave a sigh and smiled at him, she leaned over and kissed him and then got up and went to finish the meal off ready to be eaten. Scaroon looked into the fire and realised that he would have to tell Francesca the truth one day, but hoped it wasn't going to be for a long time, much had to be done now he had committed himself to the rebel cause.

All the main councillors were beginning to come together at the Pavilion where Norak lived and where they held the meetings. They were all aware of the break-in at the quarry and were very concerned what the rebels were going to use the Sycronite for.

They all settled in their seats that were in a semi-circle with Norak in the centre chair facing them, he looked around at them all wondering what their thoughts were regarding the recent event at the quarry.

Norak begun, 'Well, everyone, you are aware of the break-in at the quarry and that two cases of Sycronite was stolen. What we don't know is, what the rebels are going to use it for, but I have a strong feeling that it has something to do with the Annarki. Has anyone any thoughts concerning this latest rebel attack. We now have two more men murdered and a rebel killed, but he doesn't seem to be known by anyone.'

Voix then stood up to speak as Norak sat down, 'I have made enquiries about the dead man, and no one has any idea where he comes from. He is not local, so we can only guess he is from one of the nearby towns. If that is the case, it shows that the rebels are joining from all over the area and that the movement is getting larger and wider. We need to do something soon or we could be facing an uprising of them, and the Annarki will then get involved with their more advanced weapons and we don't need that,' he said quite adamantly.

Voix sat down and Jarvoo stood up, 'We have no idea how far this rebellion against the Annarki goes, for all we know, there might be hundreds of rebels just waiting to come out into the open to fight against the Annarki. Many are not wanting the Annarki around on this planet, in spite of them getting rid of the Greylon danger and attacks.'

Slook looked at Jarvoo and asked, 'How do you feel about the Annarki coming to our planet, Jarvoo, and living on it?'

Jarvoo was a little taken back by Slook's question, 'I for one feel we have done alright without them so far, but if they come, they come. It's all been organised now and it's too late to change it. But that doesn't change the fact that there is a rebellion building and it could get very serious and people could get killed.'

Kalock, one of the other councillors stood up next and gave a revelation that shook them all, he said, 'How do we know there isn't a spy in this room. It seems to me that the rebels are well informed and know what we are doing before we put anything into operation.'

There was a sudden silence in the room and everyone began to look round with the thought of whom it might be, if Kalock was right, or could it be Kalock saying what he'd said to throw suspicion away from himself.

The atmosphere in the room became very tense as they were pondering Kalock's point, was there a spy within their midst? Norak broke the deafening silence, 'Well, Kalock's suggestion of a spy amongst us is a little outrageous, but if that is the case, he or she will be found out and be sent to the Annarki prison moon for life, or maybe executed publically in disgrace. I will come down hard and without sympathy or mercy on anyone who betrays our people in any way.'

Norak dispersed the council and told them to watch out and listen for anything that will lead them closer to the rebels leader. As they all leave Norak's pavilion, there is a strange silence as they go and Norak can't help feeling that Kalock's suggestion scared them all and made them wonder if one of them is really a spy.

Scaroon meets the top leader of the rebels behind the market stalls where he normally meets him. He is disguised in peasants clothing with a shaggy beard and older working clothes any of the people would wear and would blend in without a problem and not be recognised. He takes Scaroon to one side in the alcove of one of the tall buildings behind the market stalls and says, 'Scaroon, we have a problem in the council, one of the councillors, Kalock has throw suspicion amongst the councillors suggesting that we have a spy amongst us. This is very dangerous. I have a feeling he thinks I am the spy and we need to get rid of him. I want you to kill him,' the council spy told him.

Scaroon looked at him in disgust, 'I'm afraid that on this occasion I detract from this murder, I will not kill a council member, it's asking too much, why don't you kill him yourself, you are closer to him and would have a better opportunity to get rid of him,' Scaroon said meaning what he'd said.

The council spy looked at him with anger, but had to remember he was in a public place and couldn't do anything physical, he was angry with Scaroon for refusing to kill Kalock, 'If I say you kill him, you kill him, do you understand,' he said with anger.

Scaroon looked him straight in the eye and said, 'If you want him dead, then you kill him. I want no part of a councillor's death, do you understand, I won't do it.'

The council spy looked at Scaroon with his anger increasing in intensity, 'Very well, Scaroon, we will talk about this matter again tomorrow, I need him out of the way before he exposes me, I'm sure he knows I am the spy. I'll meet you in front of the Corn Stores, the same time as today, don't be late, we need to get this sorted,' he said in anger and then walked away from Scaroon leaving him alone.

Scaroon was angry too and didn't trust his contact from the council, even though he was his superior in the rebel movement. He turned and went back to his horse and rode back to the Gun Club, feeling angry that he should be asked to murder a council member. He reminded himself that he was only there to begin with to find his brothers killer. He was determined to find him and eliminate him, and then decide what he was going to do from that point. Suddenly the rebel cause was not his priority; his personal revenge for his brother came first.

Scaroon walked into his Gun Club and was spoken to by one of the organising staff, he ignored the man and went to his office. The man that had spoken to him as he came in was Layham, his Gun Club Manager when he wasn't there. Layham was unsure what to do and realised that Scaroon was angry about something. Layham was one of the rebels and had a feeling that Scaroon's anger was connected to them, he knew Scaroon had gone to meet their council contact and had guessed it hadn't gone well.

Layham went to Scaroon's office and saw Scaroon sitting in his chair with his back to him, 'Scaroon, are you all right, you are obviously angry about something?'

Scaroon turned round in his chair and looked at Layham, 'Yes, I am angry, our contact in the council believes that one of the other councillors suspects him of being the spy, and he had the gall to ask me to kill him, but I refused. I am not going to kill a council member, it's too dangerous. I told him to kill him himself, but he didn't like it and stormed off before he publically hit me, I know he wanted to,' Scaroon told Layham.

Layham looked at Scaroon a little shocked, 'Well, Scaroon, I agree with you, but be careful, there are some of the rebels that would do as he asked without hesitation. But I would refuse too.'

Scaroon gave Layham a half smile, 'If there are any who want to do the job for him, then he can ask them, but it won't be me, and I appreciate your thoughts too on the matter,' Scaroon said to him.

'What are you going to do, Scaroon, he might turn on you?'

Scaroon looked at Layham, 'If he tries, or anyone else, I will cut them to pieces with my own knife, I wouldn't have a problem killing him, but not the other councillor's, I have never trusted him completely.'

'Watch your back, Scaroon, I'll keep my ear to the ground and let you know if anyone is getting to ambitious and wants to take over from you.'

'Thank you for that, Layham, I'm glad someone agrees with me, this rebel cause is getting very dangerous and I fear there maybe unrest within the rebels themselves,' Scaroon said to him.

'Yes, Scaroon, things could get very treacherous, I'll keep you informed and let you know if I hear anything,' he said and left Scaroon to his own thoughts. He was curious to see what his council contact had to say the following day.

As Scaroon was sitting in his office, he looked out of the door into the foyer of the club front. He could see five of the club members talking together and wondered what they were discussing. He stood up and went to his office door and called to them, 'Is everything alright?'

Miraka turned to answer him, 'Yes, Scaroon, we were just discussing the rota for instructing new members, we have got it organised now, don't worry, it's done.'

'Very well. I will be going shortly, will one of you close up when the last member goes home?' he asked.

Miraka nodded and Scaroon made ready to leave to go home to Francesca. His day had been quite a trial and he was ready to relax, but knew he had to disguise his anger from Francesca as he knew she would worry about him.

Chapter Thirteen

Overheard Conversations:

The following day, Scaroon set off to meet his council contact again, to try and resolve his argument from the day before. Scaroon was still adamant he wasn't going to be responsible for killing Kalok. He tied his horse up behind one of the buildings and walked down the alleyway that led to where he had arranged to meet the spy councillor.

As Scaroon is walking down the alleyway, he overhears his contact speaking to someone else. He hides by the wall just before the end of the alleyway so he can hear the conversation, he knows he is a little early, but listens to what is being said. He recognises the second man's voice as Miraka's voice and listens.

'Miraka, I want you to kill, Kalock first and then kill Scaroon, but make it look like someone from the club had done it. I no longer trust Scaroon and want him out of the way. When you have killed him, I will make you the leader in second in command after me. I think Scaroon suspects that I had something to do with his brother's murder, but that was Nigon who took care of him. We need Scaroon out of the way so he can't cause me any trouble that I suspect he will if he isn't taken care of.'

'Very well, I will pick my time and kill Scaroon and make it look like one of the Gun Club members has done it and leave evidence to suggest as such. I'll steel Layham's knife and leave it by the body of Scaroon and the blame will be set. Layham is a friend of Scaroon and does all he asks.'

'Very good, Miraka, do it as soon as you can, now go and let me know when the job has been done,' the councillor said.

Miraka left him and Scaroon held back for a few minutes and allowed himself to calm down now he knew the truth about who had killed his brother. He knew he had to play along with the Councillor just one more time. He calmed himself and then walked out of the alleyway as though he had just come down it and saw the councillor waiting for him.

Scaroon spoke first, 'Well, have you found someone to kill Kalok, I still stand by what I said yesterday?' he asked him, now knowing what the councillor had in mind.

'It's alright, Scaroon, I have sorted out the problem, Kalok will be taken care of by another man. I want you to organise the first attack on the new building site,' the councillor said to him as though everything was all right, but Scaroon now knew more than the councillor realised. He listened and played along with him.

'Very well, I will organise it when we all meet again. Is there anything else you want me to organise?' he asked the councillor.

'No, Scaroon, that is all I need you to do.'

'Very well, I will leave you, I have other business at the Gun Club,' he said and left the councillor knowing what his next move would be.

As Scaroon left the councillor and walked back down the alleyway where he came from, he knew that Miraka would kill Kalock that night and knew where he went at nighttimes, it was the Bear's Head Tavern at the north end of the town. He also knew where he could find Nigon, he was his second to call upon.

Before Scaroon went back to the Gun Club, he called in at the Gun Shop to let Francesca know he would be late home. He intended to kill, Miraka before going to wait outside of the local gym, where Nigon went every night.

As he walked into the Gun Shop, Kaleena and Francesca were talking with each other. Francesca saw Scaroon as he came in, 'Hello my love, what brings you in here today?' she asked him.

'I've called to let you know I will be late home tonight. I have some late business to take care of with a timber merchant. I'm pricing up materials to extend the Barn behind the club, but he can't get to see me until later after the Gun Club is closed, so I am going to wait for him, I'll see you when I get home,' he told her and Kaleena.

Francesca looked at him and felt a little disappointed as she had planned a special meal for him and a nice surprise after, 'That's a pity, Scaroon, I had a surprise planned for you, but I suppose it can wait. What time to you expect getting home?' she asked.

Scaroon hated telling her lies but said, 'I'm not sure, it could be quite late, but I will get home as quickly as possible,' he told her.

Kaleena couldn't help thinking that something wasn't right, but said nothing whilst he was in the shop. She knew that Francesca was disappointed, but would have to wait until he came home before giving him his surprise.

'I've got to go, I'll explain more later,' he said as he leaned over the counter and gave Francesca a kiss and then left the shop.

Francesca looked at Kaleena and they both thought that Scaroon wasn't being honest with them both. 'Francesca, do you think he was telling us the truth?' she asked her.

Francesca wasn't sure what to say, 'I'm not sure, Kaleena, but I hope it's nothing to do with the rebels, I can't help feeling it might be, I am sure he is involved with them, but if he is, what's going to be happening tonight?' she said in a questioning manner.

Kaleena walked up to Francesca and put her arm around her shoulder and said, 'We will soon find out, Francesca if he is involved with them, things are beginning to happen at the new building site with the Annarki. They are now bringing their machinery to move the earth and to begin laying the foundations.'

'I hope nothing happens to him, I now love him so much, I don't want to lose him, he has become my true love.'

Kaleena gave her a squeeze and said, 'I'm sure he will be alright, he can look after himself,' Kaleena was hoping too that Scaroon would be all right, but felt sure he was meeting someone to do with the rebels.

Miraka was waiting behind a thick bushy tree for Kalok to come past. He knew he passed this point on his way home. It wasn't long before Kalok came passed and as he did so, Miraka jumped out behind him and before Kalok knew what was happening, Miraka had slit his throat and left him to die, wiping his knife on Kalock's clothing, but left Layham's knife by him after smearing it with Kalock's blood to put the blame on him. He ran off through a woodland area into the trees and headed for the tavern as though out for a normal evening.

By the time someone had found Kalock, Miraka was in the tavern and acted, as normal, and no one knew any different.

Scaroon was waiting down the alleyway next to the Bear's Head Tavern and keeping out of sight, he knew it wouldn't be long before Miraka came out and would walk down the same alleyway he was waiting in.

His patience was rewarded and Miraka came out of the Tavern shouting good night to one of the men going home in the opposite direction, and then began to walk down the alleyway. As he walked past Scaroon, who was behind a large waste bin, Scaroon grabbed him from behind and slit his throat as Miraka had slit Kalock's earlier in the evening. As Miraka fell to the floor dead, Scaroon looked down at him and whispered, 'Sorry, Miraka, I found you first, one down, one to go.'

Scaroon didn't hesitate. He pulled Miraka's body behind the waste bin, and ran from the alleyway unseen by anyone and headed to the local Gym for his next most important victim, Nigon who had killed his brother.

He waited by the end of the building and was in disguise, and made as though he was waiting for someone. In truth, he was, but to others they didn't think he was waiting for anyone inside the gym.

Eventually, he saw Nigon come out and head across the street. Scaroon followed him and knew Nigon had to pass the local graveyard on his way home and that there would be no one else around. It was avoided by most of the people because of the dead spirits, whom they believed roamed around at night, but Nigon didn't believe in ghosts.

As Nigon walked past the graveyard, he heard someone running behind him. He turned and saw a man rushing at him. Before he could react, he felt a knife dig into his stomach and into his lungs. It only took a short time before he fell dead. Scaroon pushed him over the small graveyard wall and left him. He headed for home leaving his disguised clothing behind him near a grave that was close to the graveyard wall. He made sure he had no blood on him, and then left an unknown knife still sticking out of Nigon's torso.

He didn't waste any time in getting back to the street and walked down as though nothing had happened, but knew that the traitor councillor would know who it was that had killed Nigon and Miraka and would be looking for him.

As Scaroon headed back to Francesca's apartment, he knew he had spent his last day connected to the rebels and would have to tell Francesca the truth. He hoped she would understand and help him turn on the side of Norak and expose the real one in charge of the rebels...

He had a thought as he walked towards Francesca's apartment and decided to call on Layham and tell him that he was feeling ill and would not be at the Gun Club the following day and to ask him to run it for him until he was feeling better. Layham lived three streets away from Francesca's apartment and the detour wouldn't take long. He approached Layham's house and knocked on his door.

Layham opened his door and was followed by his son, Melando. Scaroon smiled at Melando and then at Layham, 'Hello, Layham, I have called to let you know that I seem to have picked up a stomach bug and won't be at the Gun Club for a couple of days or so, could you look after it for me until I'm feeling better?' he asked him.

Layham smiled at him, 'Yes, of course, Scaroon, it will be all right, everything is there we need, go home and get yourself well, and don't worry about the club.'

'Thank you, Layham, I appreciate your help and time. I'll be in touch, thanks again my friend, good night,' he said and left to go home to Francesca whom he'd got a lot of explaining to do to.

As he walked to Francesca's apartment, he was wondering how she would react to what he'd done and if she would stand by him. He had learned to love her very much and hoped they would be together for the rest of their lives. It all rested on how she reacted when he told her what he'd done, he decided to tell her everything and that he had killed two men that night and all were rebels including the one who had killed his brother.

He walked up to the bottom of the wooden stair case that led up to Francesca's apartment and looked up feeling hopeful he would get Francesca's help and understanding and forgive him for what he'd done over the previous weeks.

<<<<< >>>>>

As Scaroon entered Francesca's apartment, he was surprised to see Kaleena there speaking with Francesca. He looked at Kaleena with a smile, although both Kaleena and Francesca could see that Scaroon was worried about something. He tried to sound normal, but couldn't do it very well. He said to Kaleena, 'Hello, Kaleena, what brings you here tonight?'

Kaleena wasn't about to make excuses for being there and said openly, 'Well, Scaroon, Francesca asked me to come round tonight as she was concerned about you and wanted to talk to me. I can see you are not feeling your best, Scaroon, are you alright?'

Scaroon was unsure how to answer Kaleena, and sat down in his usual chair by the fire and looked back at both women. He realised that he had to tell both of them what had happened and what had been happening over the previous weeks.

'Well, Kaleena and you my dearest Francesca, I'm afraid I have some disturbing news to tell you. Francesca might have told you, Kaleena about my brother who was murdered. I came to this town to find his murderer and to kill him in revenge of his death. But something else happened as well, I learned about the rebel movement against the Annarki and joined them, in fact, they made me the leader.'

Kaleena and Francesca looked at him in shock, although they had suspected he had some connection, but not their leader. Francesca went to him, knelt in front of him, and put her hands on his knees, 'Scaroon, why didn't you tell me about this and Kaleena too?'

Scaroon looked deep into her eyes, 'I'm so sorry, Francesca, but I didn't expect falling in love with you. I am so confused.'

Kaleena looked at him and said, 'There's more isn't there, Scaroon?' she asked him. She knew he had been somewhere that night and put an end to his brother's killer's life. Have you killed your brother's murderer tonight?' she said without hesitation.

Scaroon looked at her and said, 'Yes, I have, and also a man who was going to try and kill me. I have to tell you that I know who the top leader is and that he is one of the councillors and close to Norak.'

Kaleena looked at Francesca and then back to Scaroon, 'Are you going to tell us who it is, Scaroon? I have to tell you that we have thought you had some connection to the rebels, but never thought you would be their leader.'

'I will expose the traitor of the rebels, but only when all the councillors are together. I need to be able to speak to Norak and ask his protection, I want no more to do with the rebels now I have avenged my brother. I don't like the idea of the Annarki living amongst us, but I fear the rebels more than them. The traitor in the council will know I have killed two of his helpers and will be after killing me now. I need to disappear from sight until the rebels are caught and their main leader exposed. Do you know who can help me?' he asked them not yet knowing they were part of Norak's plan to find out who the rebels are.

'Well, Scaroon,' Kaleena said, 'we have something to tell you that you are not aware of. I started the Gun Shop to hopefully attract the rebels so we could find out who they were. When you came in and told us you were starting a Gun Club, we had an idea that you might be connected to them. I will say to begin with that Francesca's love for you is real and she doesn't want anything to happen to you, she loves you very much. However, I can help you, my sister Roella, who you have met, works for Norak and is friends with his daughter. We have been keeping Norak up to date with your Gun Club, but we didn't expect you and Francesca to fall in love. But we will help you if you promise not to have anything more to do with the rebels, as you have stated you don't want to.'

Francesca then spoke to Scaroon, 'Scaroon, I love you dearly and Kaleena and I will help you keep out of the way until you can expose the traitor. Don't worry about the Annarki, we need to sort your problem out first. Once we have got the rebels arrested by Norak's security men, we can then organise for you to be at a meeting of all the councillors so you can come to them and expose the traitor.'

Kaleena then added, 'Above my shop is a room where you can stay out of the way, just in case they come to find you at Francesca's. However, I will ask Norak to set up security men around Francesca's apartment. If any rebels come here, they will be arrested immediately and thrown into the dungeons until being sent to the Annarki prison moon. I have a feeling that will make the traitor scared. Meanwhile, you and Francesca can stay in the spare room above the shop; it has all you need for the time being.'

'Thank you, Kaleena and I promise you, Francesca that no one will harm you, I will protect you to the death, I would give my life for you.'

Francesca hugged Scaroon with tears in her eyes, 'I love you so much, Scaroon, I want us to be happy and together always.'

'Don't worry my darling, we will one day be free to live and my Gun Club will be a success and be for genuine people only, no more rebels.'

Kaleena smiled at them and knew she had to act quickly. 'The dead men will not be found until tomorrow, so we will spend the night taking anything you need to my Gun Shop. Francesca and I will fetch my wagon and put all you need from here on it and take it and put everything in the room above the shop. Both of you can then stay there. I will contact Norak immediately first thing at daybreak and also ask him to have some men watch the shop in case we get any unwelcome visitors, although, Francesca and I can take care of ourselves very well. Scaroon, stay here and get things ready to put in my wagon, we won't be long.'

Francesca and Kaleena left and headed for her Gun Shop and collected her wagon. It didn't take them long to get back to Franseca's apartment and put the wagon at the bottom of the stairs that led to her rear apartment door. Scaroon had watched for them coming back and had already taken some of their things down stairs ready to put on the wagon.

It took only a short time to get everything they need packed on the wagon and they set off back to Kaleena's gun shop and parked it up at the rear of the shop where the stairs were that led to the spare room. After about an hour, they had everything set up in the new room and were feeling comfortable and safe. They planned to move everything back to Francesca's old apartment when all the trouble had been settled and the rebels were in prison on the Annarki moon.

'Kaleena, there is one man that I wish to be saved from the Annarki prison moon, that is Leyham he has been a helper to me, and a faithful friend. Can someone go to the Gun Club tomorrow and ask him to come to your shop with an excuse about new weapons or something?' he asked them.

Kaleena smiled at him, 'Yes, Scaroon, I will go myself whilst Francesca looks after the shop, it won't take me long to pick him up with my wagon.'

'Thank you again, Kaleena, I shall be forever in your debt.'

'You owe me nothing, Scaroon, just make Francesca happy when all this is sorted out, she is a good worker and I want her to be at my shop for a long time.'

'That's a task I can promise to keep,' he said with a broad smile at both women.

Chapter Fourteen

End of the Rebels:

The following morning at daybreak, Kaleena was up early and went to see Norak and Roella, she was invited in by Norak's door attendant, Paton and Roella met her in the foyer.

'Good morning, Kaleena, what has brought you here so early, it's only just after daybreak?' she asked with concern.

Kaleena was keen to speak with Roella alone and Roella took her into another room away from the foyer where they could speak, 'Roella, when will Norak be up and around?'

'Very soon, Kaleena, but if it is urgent, I can ask Shalaine, his daughter, to go and wake him up.'

'Well, Roella, I have major news about the rebels, Scaroon told us about his involvement with them and I need to tell Norak as soon as I can, I have to get back to the shop.'

'Very well, Kaleena, I will go and tell Shalaine now, I think she is getting up.'

'Thank you, Roella, I will wait here for you,' Kaleena said eager to let Norak know her news.

Roella disappeared into the other rooms and shortly brought Shalaine back with her, Kaleena had no hesitation in telling her, her reason for being there, 'Shalaine, I need you to go and wake your father, I have urgent news for him concerning the rebels, it's crucial he knows what I know immediately.'

'Very well, Kaleena, I will go to him now and tell him, I'm sure he will come right away,' she said and went to wake her father.'

It wasn't long before Norak came back with Sharlaine and was curious to hear what Kaleena had found that was so urgent to come at such an early hour. 'Hello, Kaleena, what is this news that is so important about the rebels?' he asked her with concern in his voice.

Kaleena began to tell Norak her news and about what had happened the previous night. 'Norak, you know that we had suspected Scaroon of being connected with the rebels and that he came to our town to find out who killed his brother. Well, he found out who had killed him and also a man who was going to kill him too. I have to tell you that he dealt with them accordingly and both men are dead and that they were also rebels. He told us that he had been leading the rebels under instruction and orders from a traitor within your high council.'

Norak looked at her in shock, 'So, how is Francesca taking all this?' he asked her with great concern and worry.

'Francesca is taking it very well. After Scaroon came back last night, after killing the two rebels, he told us all about what he'd found out and asked us to speak to you and to say he wants to speak to you himself. He is prepared to give you the names of all the rebels and expose the main leader in the High Council, but he asks that you don't take action against him for helping you.'

'If he can expose the main man in the councillors and gives us the names of the rebels, I will happily overlook his actions, but he is in danger now from the high council traitor, he will know it's Scaroon who has killed the two other men and will be after him. He needs protecting from the traitor,' Norak said with concern.

Kaleena smiled at him, 'I have taken care of that for the moment, Scaroon and Francesca have moved into the spare room over my shop. However, there is one man that Scaroon wants saving from the rebels, he is called Layham, who has helped him and been a close friend and ally. I am going to the Gun Club later to pick him up and take him back to my shop. He can stay there whilst the other rebels are arrested by your security. I also would like you to post some security near Francesca's apartment and around my shop, just in case they come looking for Scaroon.'

'That is not a problem, Kaleena we should be able to arrest them if they come looking for either Scaroon or Francesca.' Norak looked at Roella, 'Roella, go back with Kaleena to her shop and stay there whilst Kaleena comes back from fetching Scaroon's friend from the Gun

Club, I don't like the idea of Francesca being alone, even though Scaroon will be upstairs in the spare room.'

'Very well, Norak, I'll be happy to stay with Francesca, I also know she has learned her unharmed fighting skills very well and would easily deal with anyone attacking her,'

'That is as it might be, Roella, but they might come with Guns and get very desperate,' Norak said then looked at Kaleena, 'Kaleena, tell Scaroon to make a list of all the rebels and where to find them, and tell him I will go to the shop in disguise later today to speak with him. The sooner we arrest all the rebels the better. I will then arrange a meeting of the high council and let Scaroon point out the traitor.'

'That's a good plan, Norak, we will go back now and get ready for you coming and I'll go to the Gun Club and pick up Layham. It might be an idea to have the Gun Club closed for a day or two until everything has been sorted out, and the rebels are caught and locked up. I will stay with Layham until he has locked it up and then we will go back to my shop.'

'That's good enough, Kaleena, I will come to your shop sometime around mid day, let Scaroon know so he can make me a list of the rebels.'

'Very well, Norak, we will go now and get sorted and prepared. I think there are going to be a good number of rebels rounded up today. I for one will feel better when they are on their way to the Annarki prison moon,' Kaleena said.

152

<<<<< >>>>>

Kaleena and Roella set off back to Kaleena's shop and waited until it was time for Kaleena to go to Scaroon's Gun Club to pick up Layham. They chatted as they rode back to the Gun Shop.

'Kaleena, how are Francesca and Scaroon getting on with each other?' she asked.

'They are very much in love, but Scaroon is concerned for Francesca, he doesn't want the rebels to come after her, that is why we have moved them into my spare room above the shop, they should be safe there until all the rebels have been arrested. The sooner it's all done with the better we'll all be,' Kaleena said.

'Do you realise, Kaleena that if Francesca and Scaroon hadn't have got together, we would never have found out who the rebels were and the traitor in the high council,' she said.

'That is true, Roella, it's sometimes strange how things work out, it's the power of love in this case, and believe me, they are very much in love and I'm happy for them,' Kaleena added.

As they walked into the Gun Shop, Francesca was standing behind the counter with Scaroon watching from the back of the shop and out of sight of anyone coming in, but they could speak to each other when no one was in the shop.

153

Francesca was pleased to see Roella, 'Good morning, Roella, how are you today?' she asked with a smile.

'I am alright, Francesca, but more to the point, how are you and Scaroon?' Roella asked her back.

'We are fine now things are in the open; I am relieved that Scaroon told Kaleena and I the truth last night. We can now hope that the whole rebel business is going to be cleared up and everyone can get on with their lives again,' Francesca told her.

'Yes, that is true, Francesca, it shouldn't take long now we know the rebels are going to be caught at last.' Roella shouted to Scaroon in the back of the shop who was listening to their conversations, 'Scaroon, can you come to the side door?' she asked him.

Scaroon walked to the door and said, 'What is it, Roella?'

Norak is happy to forget your killing of the two men, but he wishes you to make a list of the rebels and where to find them, apart from your friend, Layham. He will arrange a meeting with the council so you can expose the traitor too. He is very pleased you have come clean,' Roella told him.

'Very well, Roella, I will make a list for him right now and he can have it when I see him.'

'That is good, Scaroon, he is going to call at the shop around midday. You can speak with him in the room upstairs where you and Francesca are staying for the moment.'

Thank you, Roella, I will look forward to speaking with him, I need to clear a few other things up with him too. I want all this out of the way so Francesca and I can enjoy our lives together for a very long time.'

Francesca smiled over to him, 'So do I, Scaroon, so do I.'

They all chuckled at Francesca's comment and Francesca went and made them all a hot drink and they sat in the back of the shop until it was time to open it and for Kaleena to go to the Gun Club to pick up Layham.

<<<<< >>>>>

Kaleena walked into the Gun Club and saw a man standing by a row of long-bows and arrows, she guessed he was probably Layham, He turned and saw her walk in and recognised her, even though she didn't recognise him immediately.

'Good morning, Kaleena, how are you today?' he asked.

'I'm fine, - are you Layham, Scaroons friend and helper?' she asked. There was no one else around yet as it was a little too early for any members to come.

He smiled at her, 'Yes, I am, why do you ask?'

'I have instructions from Norak, you are to close the club down for a few days and I want you to come

155

with me to my Gun Shop. Scaroon is there with Francesca, and Norak is calling later. Scaroon has important news for you.'

'Really, he called last night to say he was not well and asked me to look after the Gun Club for a few days, is he feeling better?'

Kaleena smiled at what he said, 'I will tell you on the way to my shop, so can you close the club and leave a notice that the Gun Club will be closed for a few days?' she told him.

Although Layham was very curious, he did as Kaleena had asked and closed everything down and locked up and left a notice on the club's outer door saying the club was closed until the end of the week, which was another four days.

As they rode back to town and to Kaleena shop, she explained to Layham what had happened and what was to happen. Layham was shocked to hear about Scaroon killing Miraka and Nigon, but understood when she explained his reasons and was pleased that Scaroon had spared him from the security people. He was in full support of what Scaroon was going to do.

When they got back to Kaleena's shop Layham was shown upstairs to where Scaroon was relaxing and waiting for Norak to come and see him. When he heard Layham's voice coming up the stairs and talking to Kaleena, he stood up and greeted his friend, 'Hello, Layham, I'm glad you came. I take it that Kaleena has explained what's happened.'

Before Layham could answer, Kaleena spoke first, 'Yes, Scaroon, I have explained everything and Layham is in full support of your actions.'

Layham smiled at Scaroon and they shook hands as friends and sat down. Layham asked, 'So it was Nigon who killed your brother then?' he asked Scaroon.

'Yes, Layham, my reason for being in this town was to find my brother's murderer and deal with him appropriately, which I did.'

'In which case, he got what he deserved,' Layham said.

They chatted for a while and had a drink of wine that Kaleena had brought them. She was waiting also for Norak to arrive. Just before midday, a stranger walked in the shop with a hooded cowl over his head and looked like a holy man of some kind. He walked up to the counter and Francesca spoke to him, she wasn't sure who he was, but had an idea.

'Good day, sir, can I help you,' she said hoping it was Norak in disguise.

From under his cowl he said, 'Yes, Francesca, it's me, Norak, I have come to meet with Scaroon,' he said freely as there was no one in the shop at that time.

Francesca sighed with relief and showed Norak through the shop and up the stairs to the spare room. She left him with Scaroon and Layham. Kaleena came back down stairs with Francesca and joined Roella in the shop. Business was a little slow in the shop, but business that was more important, was being discussed upstairs.

Norak sat down with Layham and Scaroon and he looked over at Scaroon and said, 'Well, Scaroon, I am pleased you have decided to help us. I'm sorry to have heard about your brother being murdered, but I understand you got your revenge for him?'

Scaroon gave a slight grin at Norak, 'Yes, Norak, but that is personal, I have more news for you. I have made you a list of the rebels that are active and need to be arrested by your security. I also know who the traitor is in your high councillors, but I wish to be there myself to expose him. I suggest that the day I do that that all of your doors are supported with guards outside, in case he tries to make a run for it when he is exposed.'

Norak looked at Scaroon with interest, 'Scaroon, I have to admit you are a bit of a mystery. Although you are exposing the traitor for us, and have given me the list of the rebels, I know you still have feelings about the Annarki joining our people. What have you against them?'

Scaroon scanned Norak with a blank look, 'Well, Norak, I have never felt comfortable around alien people, but I have done what I came here to do, and that is avenge my brother. However, I hadn't banked on falling madly in love with Francesca. I am prepared to try and get on with the Annarki and live my life and run my business. I also hope to officially mate with

158

Francesca when all this rebellion is over and they are on their way to the Annarki prison moon. Apart from my friend, Layham, here, I never felt comfortable with the rebels, even though I finished-up being their direct leader after your traitor. All I want now is a happy life with Francesca and to run my Gun Club officially as an ongoing business. There is one thing you must do, Norak, it is vital that you arrest the rebels today as they plan to go to the Annarki site and blow up some of the foundations and the ground moving machines. They will be going after dark so you need to act fast through today,' he told Norak with urgency in his voice.

Norak smiled at him, 'Well, Scaroon, I think that will soon be put into practice. The men you killed last night will be found today and be buried immediately, but as you will know, the traitor in the high council will be looking for you, so stay here until we arrested the rebels.'

'I will, Norak, don't worry, I have a feeling that it won't take you long to gather the rebels together and that you will have them all in your dungeon before nightfall. I will then feel safer.'

'I think we all will, Scaroon, I will take your list and put the plan into action to get the rebels arrested immediately I leave here, we shall then make arrangements for you to come to our meeting and expose the traitor.'

'That sounds good, Norak, but I think the high council are in for a surprise, it needs to be sorted soon and I look forward to exposing him, it was he that organised the death of my brother, and the Annarki prison moon is perfect for him and goodbye to him for the rest of his life.'

'Worry not, Scaroon, we shall have all the rebels arrested before nightfall and soon we will give you the chance to expose the traitor. I can assure you that the Annarki site will remain intact.'

'Good, Norak, we will wait here until we hear from you and know that all the rebels are locked up. Tell your men to take weapons with them, some of the rebels carry handguns with them and will try and use them. I hope none of your security officers get hurt or worse.'

'I will pass that information on, Scaroon, they will be very careful, they are well trained. I'll send word as soon as we have them all in prison.'

'Thank you, Norak, I hope all goes well.'

Norak smiled at Scaroon and said, 'I also thank you, Scaroon, your help is going to save much trouble coming to us, I will see you later.'

Norak left and took the list of the rebels with him. They were all quickly arrested and thrown into the pavilion dungeons some, were picked up from outside Francesca's apartment before they could get to her door and break in, to hopefully get to Scaroon and Francesca. Francesca and Scaroon would soon be going back to live there and getting on with their lives.

Chapter fifteen

Confidence is High:

After Norak had left Scaroon and Layham, they spoke of things to come, Scaroon was now looking forward to running his Gun Club officially and not being a front to the rebels. He was going to make it the largest in the area and maybe consider expanding to other towns.

Scaroon looked across to Layham, 'Thank you, Layham for your help and support at the club. I know you were not happy with the rebel situation and I didn't really want to become their leader, but it was a means to an end for me to find out who killed my brother, now that is taken care of, Francesca and I can plan our future.'

'I am pleased for you, Scaroon and I will help all I can at the gun club. We can promote it now and build a genuine membership up with no rebel involvement,' Layham said.

'That is true my friend and I will be making you the official manager to work with me and pay you well for it. It is one way I can say thank you for your past support to me.'

'That is very generous of you, Scaroon, but I enjoy working there and hope to be with you for as long as I can be.'

'That is good, my friend, I now know it's all going to work out and I'd like you to be my man of honour when Francesca and I are officially mated, would you like that?' he asked Layham.

'I would be honoured, Scaroon, I hope it's soon.'

Norak wasted no time in organising his security officers and they began to arrest the rebels one by one and had little resistance as they were caught by surprise. Some of them tried to escape using their handguns, but two were killed by the security force and three were injured by the security laser guns. One of the security men was slightly injured by a shoulder wound, but would soon recover.

By early evening, all the rebels on the list were arrested and were now locked up in the dungeons beneath the pavilion. Norak went down to them to see all the rebels that had been arrested and they were shouting all kinds of abuse at him. One of them shouted, 'Where is Scaroon, he is our leader?'

Norak saw an opportunity to make them think that Scaroon was still one of them. He looked round at them all and answered the man's question, 'Scaroon has escaped, but worry not, he will be found and will be executed there and then. As for you lot, you will be shortly be taken to the Annarki prison moon, you will never leave there and cause me any trouble again, such are the rewards of rebellion,' he told them all.

'There is one you haven't caught though, he is the main leader, you'll never know who he is,' one of the rebels shouted.

Norak turned and looked at the man who had shouted, 'We shall have to wait and see, don't underestimate my security men, the traitor will be found and will probably be joining you.'

All the rebels began shouting more abuse at Norak, but he just turned and left them to await their fate.

Later that day, Norak disguised himself again and went to see Scaroon and Francesca. Layham was with them, and it had been decided that he was going to take over Kaleena's room permanently when Scaroon and Francesca went back to Francesca's apartment. Layham was a single parent with his son Melando, but hoped to find someone at some later stage after everything had been settled with the rebels and the new city was begun.

Norak went into the room and joined them, Kaleena was with them also and was pleased to see Norak and hoped he brought good news. 'Good evening, Norak,' Kaleena said as he came in and sat down with them, 'I hope you had no trouble arresting the rebels.'

He smiled at them all, 'I am pleased to say that everyone was apprehended, but three were killed by the security men, they tried to fire on them, but were not lucky to hit any of our people, other than one who was injured by a bullet in his shoulder, but he is going to be alright,' he told them.

'I'm pleased to hear that, Norak,' Scaroon said as he cuddled Francesca on his knee.

They were all happy to hear Norak's news. Norak smiled over to Scaroon and said, 'When we had apprehended them all and locked them up, I made a space transmission to Barook, the Annarki leader. At the top of my Pavilion, I have a very powerful transmitter that I can use to contact them with. I spoke to Barook personally and he says he is very pleased to hear that you helped us, Scaroon, and looks forward to speaking with you very soon.'

Scaroon looked at Norak a little shocked, 'You mean, Barook wishes to speak to me in person? But he is the main leader of the Annarki, that is amazing,' Scaroon said still trying to take Norak's words into his head.

Francesca looked at Scaroon with a broad smile, 'That is fantastic, Scaroon, you are going to be thanked by the Annarki leader himself. I am so proud of you,' she said as she gave him a full kiss on his mouth.

They all chuckled at Francesca's reaction and were pleased for Scaroon's future meeting with Barook. Scaroon looked round at them all, 'Well, everyone, I expected a tap on the back from the council after exposing the traitor, but not actually meeting Barook himself. I'm so amazed and happy.'

Norak looked at him, 'Scaroon, I think after you have spoken to Barook himself, you'll have no more concerns about the Annarki coming to this planet.'

Scaroon smiled at Norak, 'I hope not, Norak, but I will have a few questions to ask him,' he said with a grin.

'I've no doubt you will have, Scaroon, and I'm sure he will answer them precisely for you and assure you that you have nothing to worry about. However, before we organise the meeting where you can expose the traitor, I have to go to the Annarki home planet to discuss the building project with the Annarki council there. When I get back, I will arrange a meeting of my high councillors and it's then that you can expose the traitor. He or she will be now aware we have arrested the rebels and will be getting very worried.

'I am being picked up by an Annarki space ship tomorrow with some of my councillors, if he or she is amongst them that go with me, it might be the case that the traitor might give him or herself away, but I will be watching out to see what happens. I am going to suggest that Barook comes back with us to Thaldernian, but unknown to my councillors that come back with me. He will hopefully keep out of sight until the day of the meeting when we find out who the traitor is.'

'I like the sound of that, Norak, it will be a shock to the traitor to find out Barook is there, I suggest that he stays out of sight until I make my announcement, then he can come and tell the traitor where he is going for the rest of his life.'

Norak noticed that Scaroon said, "He", 'Am I to take it Scaroon that the traitor is a man, seeing as you've just referred to him as "He".

Scaroon nodded to him, 'Yes, Norak, but that is all I will say until his exposure, if you don't mind.'

'That is fine by me, Scaroon, I will look forward to it.'

They all nodded and were looking forward to the exposure of the traitor; it wouldn't be long before he was known to them.

The following morning at 9am, a large dark coloured Annarki ship landed on the ground behind Norak's pavilion. Norak, Voix, Slook, Garoo and Pleena were there waiting for it and saw it coming from a good distance away. As it landed, Norak wasn't sure whether Barook would come with it or not. As it settled down, the lower door opened and set itself on the ground creating a ramp to allow anyone to walk up into the ship.

Pleena, was the only woman councillor that was going with them, and was first to walk on board, being followed by the four men. They were shown to the flight deck where they took their seats ready for the flight back to Annarki. Although the new tachyon engines were now fitted on all the Annarki ships, they still had their usual drives that were used for interplanetary travel. The tachyon drives were only going to be used for interstellar journeys.

Barook hadn't come with the ship and soon they were taking off to go back to Annarki. Everyone seemed happy, but Voix seemed a little nervous. 'Are you alright, Voix?' Norak asked him.

Voix looked at him with a blank expression, 'Yes, I'm alright, Norak, I'm just a little nervous about travelling in space, it's my first time.'

Norak laughed at him warmly, 'I can assure you it is safe and we will be at Annarki in no time at all. These spaceships can travel very fast and it will only take us a few hours to reach the Annarkian planet, just relax and enjoy the trip.'

Voix just gave a slight grin, tried to settle down, and said very little. He knew that it was the first time for all the others apart from Norak, he had been into space a few times over the years and knew he had been to Annarki before on at least two occasions.

As they began to leave Thaldernian, the rear view was shown on one of the control room's monitors and they watch with interest as they left Thaldernian way behind them, although Voix was still unsure about being on board a spacecraft for the first time. Other than Voix, they enjoyed their flight to Annarki and soon they were approaching the planet.

As their spacecraft moved into the atmosphere of Annarki, Norak stood up and looked at the front outer viewer that gave a panoramic view of the planet's surface and all the amazing buildings. Pleena stood up and joined him and watched as they moved closer to the vast city complex that in fact covered the whole planet. Annarki had two main seas, but two thirds of Annarki was land and split into two major landmasses.

Pleena watched with interest with Norak and the others came to observe as they saw the gigantic buildings reaching to the sky that defied gravity. The Annarki building technology was very futuristic and showed many buildings, both high and low of many different shapes and designs. The one they were heading for was a giant dome that covered a large area. This was the planet's headquarters and where Barook resided with his councillors, just as Norak lived in his pavilion, although Norak's councillors lived in different places around their Thaldernian city. Voix remained in his seat until the ship came to rest on a large landing bay that stuck out from the side of the dome. He hadn't enjoyed their journey one bit, but was glad the spaceship had come to a rest, but dreaded the thought of going back to Thaldernian on the return trip.

As they alighted from the spaceship, they were greeted by Barook, 'Good day to you all, it's good to see you, we shall be holding the meeting this evening and then you can relax at one of our leisure complexes. I'm sure you will find it very welcoming,' he said to them.

Norak spoke with a wide smile, 'It's good to be here again, Barook, but I'm afraid Voix is not a good space traveller,' he said as they looked back at him.

Barook smiled at Voix, 'You will soon get used to it, Voix, and rest well here and enjoy what is on offer before returning home to Thaldernian.'

Voix forced a smile and answered, 'Thank you, Barook, I will do my best, I guess I'm not good at flying in space,' he said back to him.

Norak and Barook chuckled at him and they continued to the restroom where they enjoyed a well-cooked meal and relaxed.

Later after relaxing for the afternoon, they were shown to the meeting room where all the Annarkian councillors were gathered. Norak and his councillors sat along with them and Barook was sitting next to Norak with Voix to Norak's right.

When everyone was settled, Barook stood up and turned to look round at everyone. 'Well, everyone, we are here to discuss the building of our first major city on Thaldernian. We hope to build several in different parts of the planet and help Norak's people advance another stage from where they are now. Norak and I have discussed this project at great length and many new facilities will be available to the Thaldernian people. Over the coming years, we hope to see the Neanderthal race become integrated with ours and live in peace and harmony together. We have already taken some of our earth-moving machines to Thaldernian and have begun clearing the site for the first city.'

Barook then turned and waved his hands in a wide sweep in front of a large wall behind him, moments later, a large projection appeared on the wall that showed the artist's impression of what the city would look like. Norak and his councillors, and even Voix looked at it with great interest.

'That looks amazing, Barook,' Pleena commented.

Barook turned to her with a smile, 'Thank you, Pleena, we hope all your people will appreciate what we want to do for them. We have many things to teach you that will advance your present knowledge a great deal. The new city will contain new educational centres for all ages, and adults and children will be able to learn new things and put them into practice.'

Norak and his four councillors looked at the projected scene of the proposed city and were in awe of what was to be built on Thaldernian.

Slook was curious, 'Barook, how long will this city take to build?'

Barook grinned at him, 'It should take less than one of your planet's years. Our building technology will make the city possible very quickly and soon your people will be able to come to it and some will be able to live there if they so choose.'

'That will be good to see, Barook, I for one will welcome it and look forward to living in it with my family.'

Barook nodded to him, 'That is good, Slook, we hope many will come and live there. We shall have many places where families can live and grow. The city will also create new work for your people and hopefully bring many more from other towns around where you live.'

Norak smiled and added, 'I'm sure our people will be waiting to join the workforce and help to build the city.'

Barook smiled at Norak, 'This is what we hope for, Norak. There will be many opportunities for your people to learn new skills.

Barook waved his hand over the projected city again and began to show them various proposed buildings that were to be used for different purposes, even Voix was amazed at the things to come. He had settled down from his space trip and now felt comfortable.

When the meeting was over, they were shown to their temporary quarters to stay in whilst they were there.

The following day they were given a tour of the vast city and shown the more important and impressive sights. Barook had made sure their stay was as pleasant as

171

possible before they were to go home to Thaldernian the following day. Everyone enjoyed the two days, but Voix wasn't looking forward to the journey back home to his own world and would be glad once he'd got back and was walking on familiar ground.

Later that evening, Norak went and called on Voix to see how he was doing. Voix was listening to some calming classical music and relaxing and mentally gearing himself up for his journey home.

Norak pressed his communications button on the outside of his apartment and Voix told the automatic door command to let him in.

'Good evening, Voix, am I disturbing you?' he asked.

'No, Norak, I was just relaxing and listening to some nice classical music on the Annarki music system, that is one thing I'll look forward too when the city is built.'

Norak and Voix sat down in the very comfortable chairs that were in the apartments and faced each other. Norak asked, 'Well, Voix, what do you think to all the things that Barook showed us yesterday?'

Voix looked with a blank expression, 'I think what they have proposed is very good, I hope our people will accept it all. Now the rebels are in prison, we can look forward to a peaceful transition to what the Annarki are going to do. However, please, Norak, don't invite me

172

here again, or anywhere that means travelling in outer space, it's not for me.'

Norak laughed at him, 'Very well, Voix, I will keep that in mind, I guess not everyone likes the adventure of space travel.'

Voix nodded his head, 'Yes, Norak, especially me.'

'So, Voix, what is your favourite aspect of the new city we are going to have built?' Norak asked him.

'I think all the educational buildings, that is going to help our people become more educated and skilled in many ways, the children will be educated to a higher degree too,' he said with a reserved enthusiasm.

'I agree with you, Voix, we are not only going to learn much new technology like they have here, but the educational system is going to be wonderful for all the children at different ages. I also like the transport system they have here, the hovering transporters are amazing. Barook told me that they work on a similar system to their spacecraft and use something he calls Anti-gravity.'

'Yes, Norak, there are going to be many changes. It almost makes my head spin.'

Norak and Voix chatted for most of the evening, the main topic being the new city. Norak eventually went back to his own apartment and settled down for the night.

Chapter Sixteen

The Spy is Exposed:

The following morning, all five of the Thaldernians were taken back to the spacecraft's landing bay and they all walked aboard ready to go back to Thaldernian. Voix was, as expected, very apprehensive about the flight, but Norak assured him it wouldn't be long before they reached Thaldernian again and his anxiety would be over.

They all settled into their seats in the control room and shortly afterwards they lifted up and headed towards outer space. Voix was sitting quietly and pondering all that had been said at the meeting with Barook.

The other four were enjoying the view from the front viewer and watched as the spaceship left Annarki. Voix remained sat in his seat.

It was only a matter of hours before they reached Thaldernian and were soon settling down on the land behind Norak's pavilion. Voix was the first to alight from the spaceship and gave a deep sigh of relief. He looked at the others and said, 'Next time you go into space, please leave me behind, I'm going home,' he said and turned and headed for his own house. All the others chuckled to themselves after enjoying the flight there and back from Annarki.

After they had all gone back to their individual homes, Norak was sitting in his private chamber and was expecting a visitor. Unknown to everyone else on the flight back from Annarki, Barook had remained out of sight in a private cabin. He wanted to be there with some of his own security along with Norak's when the traitor was exposed, but remain outside the council room until the right moment.

Scaroon and Francesca were preparing to move back into Francesca's apartment, and were glad that the rebels were no longer around, 'I'm glad we are going back to your apartment, Francesca,' Scaroon said to her, 'I have got used to it and feel at home there now.'

'Yes, me too, Scaroon, Layham can then settle into this smaller apartment and make himself at home with his son, Melando.' Francesca answered his comment.

Layham had gone to fetch his son from their old place, Melando was sixteen years old and a bright lad and hoped to work with his father at the Gun Club, but was waiting until everything had settled down with the up-evils of the rebels and the new city before asking Scaroon if he could help at the Club.

'I hope Layham settles down alright now that the rebels are out of the way,' Francesca said. Scaroon was just putting the last of the bedding into a large box ready to carry down the stairs and put onto Kaleena's wagon.

'Yes, Francesca, I'm sure he will and I think that Melando will be more relaxed, I don't think he liked his father being a member, I know that Layham had told him, just in case anything went wrong. He had instructed Melando to come to see Kaleena should anything have happened to him and explain why he had come to her. Layham had been in the Gun Shop a few times with Melando for things of his own and had bought Melando a set of Archery equipment. Melando had met Kaleena a few times and got on with her very well.

'Well, Melando won't have to worry anymore about his father; things are going to be much happier for everyone now.'

As they were preparing to take their stuff down to the cart, Norak came up to them, but he was now dressed as he would, normally be, there was no need any more for him to be in disguise.

As he walked into the room, Scaroon saw him first, 'Good day to you, Norak, did your trip to Annarki go well?' he asked.

'Yes, Scaroon, it went very well and things are moving along nicely in the right direction too. But I have come to tell you that the meeting for the council is tomorrow night, are you able to come?'

'Oh yes, Norak, I'm ready, but I feel that I should be in disguise when everyone meets, it will make the other councillors wonder who I am, especially the traitor.'

'That sounds a good idea, Scaroon, I'll leave it to you how you want to appear to everyone. At the right moment, I will tell the councillors that we have a special guest, they will probably think it's Barook, but we know that won't be true, in any case, Barook is a larger person, so they will be unsure what to think, especially the traitor.'

Scaroon chuckled at Norak, 'Yes, the traitor is in for the shock of his life, I can't wait, to expose him, especially now I know that he organised the death of my brother, he is going to get his just dues, and very soon.'

Francesca looked at Scaroon and could see by the look on his face that he was going to get great satisfaction in exposing the traitor, 'Scaroon, what will you do if the traitor attacks you? He is going to be horrified at his revelation of being known as a traitor.'

'I hope he does, Francesca, it will give me an excuse to kill him myself, but I feel that he won't dare, there will be too many people around him to stop him, let alone the security guards that will be ready to grab him.'

Norak smiled at Scaroon, 'Yes, Scaroon, he's little chance of getting at you; he will be apprehended very quickly,' Norak assured him.

As they were talking, Layham and Melando came into the apartment and saw Norak there, 'Hello, Norak, how did your trip go?' he said and then looked at Melando, 'This is Melando, my son, he is sixteen and a bright lad.'

Norak smiled at them and said, 'Well, Layham, my trip went very well, things are going to get started very soon in the new city,' he then looked at Melando and shook his hand, Melando was nearly as tall as Layham. 'Hello, Melando it's nice to meet you, you are a big lad for sixteen, what are your plans for the future?' Norak asked him.

Melando smiled back at Norak, 'Well sir, I was hoping that Scaroon might find me a job working with my father,' he said then looking across at Scaroon.

They were all listening to him, Norak smiled at Scaroon, 'Well, Scaroon, can you find Melando a job at the Gun Club?'

Scaroon laughed heartily, 'I'm sure we can find you a job there, Melando, now the rebels are out of the way, I have a few jobs that will be available, and you can have your choice.'

Melando went to Scaroon and gave him a hug, 'Thank you, Scaroon, I am a hard worker like my Dad, you won't be sorry,' he said as he stepped back again.

Everyone laughed warmly at Melando reaction to Scaroon's words and were pleased that Scaroon would give him a job at the Gun Club. Melando was very pleased with himself and his question to Scaroon came a little quicker than he had planned.

Layham tapped Melando on his shoulder, 'So it seems you are going to be working with me, Son, I'm sure you'll do just fine.'

<<<<< >>>>>

All the councillors were gathering in the usual meeting room, including Scaroon in his disguise. He was dressed with a habit type looking garment that covered his clothes beneath it. The hood was partially covering his face so no one could see him properly. All the councillors were mumbling between each other and wondering who the stranger was. Scaroon took his seat next to Norak at the front of everyone. The seating had been slightly arranged differently, that left Scaroon and Norak sitting partially by themselves from the others.

When they had all settled, everyone's eyes were on Scaroon, but they had no idea who the stranger was. Norak stood up to address the council members, 'Good evening everyone, tonight we have a special guest with us, in fact we have two special guests.'

At that moment, the automatic door to the meeting room opened and no other that Barook walked in. Although Scaroon couldn't see Barook, he guessed who it would be and looked forward to speaking to him later after the exposure had been done.

Norak continued, 'The last time we all met, Kalock suggested that we might have a traitor amongst us. Sadly, Kalock was murdered the day after the meeting, it seems that he was right and the traitor was scared that Kalock would expose him. However, there is another with us who knows the true identity of the traitor.'

Everyone looked round and there was one amongst them feeling very nervous, but didn't move a muscle and hoped that whoever this stranger was had got it wrong. Norak looked round at everyone and glanced at Barook before resting his eyes on Scaroon.

Norak then said, 'I will now call on our guest sitting by me to speak his words and settle this mystery once and for all.

Scaroon stood up and uncovered his face and removed his facial disguise of a long beard and moustache, he then looked over at Voix, who had now gone a very pale shade of white. Scaroon just lifted his hand and pointed at Voix, 'There is your traitor, Voix, he was also responsible for the death of my brother.'

Voix stood up in a rage and said, 'This is not true, Scaroon lies.'

Norak then realised that Voix had given himself away, everyone was shocked at the revelation by Scaroon, Norak looked at Voix and said, 'If Scaroon is lying, how come you know his name, no one else does and has never met him. You are guilty, Voix and I trusted you as my second in command.'

Voix tried to run for the door but was stopped by Barook. Voix was able to push past Barook, but only just. As the automatic door opened, he was met with security guards from Norak's men and those from Annarki who had come with Barook. He was seized and grabbed very tightly and couldn't move, 'You stupid Neanderthals, can't you see that the Annarki only want us to be their slaves and then throw us out of their precious damned city, you will be sorry.'

Norak looked at Voix and said, 'Voix, were you are going, you won't have to worry about working with the Annarkians, I hope you enjoy yet another space trip, but this time you will be going to the prison moon, a one way trip.'

Scaroon then walked over to where he was being held by the Annarki guards, 'Voix, I overheard you telling Miraka that you organised the death of my brother, and also he was to kill me as well as Kalock. You are going to go where you deserve to be. I can assure you, you are lucky, I nearly came to kill you along with Miraka and Nigon. I only accepted the position you gave me as leader of the rebels so I could find out who killed my brother, now you are going to pay for it for the rest of your life, good bye traitor.' Scaroon said and then asked Barook, 'Barook, may I do one last thing before we all depart?'

Barook smiled at him and answered, 'Be my guest, Scaroon,' having a good idea what was going to happen.

Suddenly, Scaroon turned round with his fist clenched and hit Voix straight and full on his nose and flattened it to his face and broke it in no uncertain terms. Voix's blood splattered all over the place and unfortunately was splashed on the guards that was holding him. Scaroon looked at Voix and said, 'Think yourself lucky, Voix, if I had have been in the street, I would have put my knife straight through your black heart, but I held back so you would receive a punishment more worthy of you. Have fun on the prison moon.' Scaroon looked at the guards that had had blood splashed on them and said, 'I'm sorry about that men, send the cleaning bill to Voix's account, he will no doubt be paying for it.' The guards just smiled at Scaroon and nodded with a grin.

Barook smiled at Scaroon, 'Scaroon, remind me not to get on your wrong side,' he said and grinned at him and chuckled with a throaty growl.

Scaroon just smiled back at him and looked back at Voix, 'As for you, Voix, your mistake was having my brother killed, you signed your death warrant from that moment on as I don't think you'll live very long where you are going.'

Norak walked up to Voix and added, 'Voix, you are a fool, you could have been the next council leader after me, now you will lead no one, only your own pitiful thoughts.'

The Annarki guards took Voix away with him screaming abuse and death wishes that were not going to do him any good. When they had left, Barook walked over to where Norak and Scaroon were standing. Barook looked round at the rest of the councillors and motioned for them to sit down, as they had stood up in shock at Scaroon's revelation of Voix. They were all in shock at the news and never thought it would have been their second councillor.

Barook looked round at everyone and then at Scaroon and said, 'Scaroon, you have done this council a great service exposing Voix. He has indeed been found out and will pay for it for as long as he lives,' he then looked at the other councillors and said, 'we are not here to make slaves of you, in fact we have many great things to offer you and teach you. Our aim is to advance your technology many times over and make the Neanderthals part of our society.'

Barook then looked at Scaroon once more and offered him his hand to shake it, Scaroon stood up and smiled at Barook, 'Thank you, my Lord Barook, I must admit that I once wondered what the true intentions were of the Annarki, but I no longer doubt you and look forward to working with you where I can.'

Barook smiled at him, 'Well, I'm glad you now think that way, Scaroon, because we want to make you a city councillor once it is finished, you have earned the position and have save many lives from being lost. None of the rebels will bother you or anyone else again.'

Scaroon was lost for words, but was able to say, 'I am honoured, My Lord Barook, and will look forward to serving on your council for the new city.'

'You have earned it, Scaroon, we shall speak more of it later,' Barook said and then looked at everyone else in the room, 'may I say here and now, if anyone else causes any trouble for yours or my people, they will suffer the same fate as the rebels and Voix, on this point, Norak and I are in agreement.'

Suddenly the automatic door opened and Francesca, Kaleena, Layham and Melando came in. Francesca went to Scaroon and hugged him. They all shook hands with each other and then Norak said,

183

'Please everyone, I have another announcement to make, I have decided that Layham and Kaleena are also going to be members of this high council to replace Kalock and Voix. Kaleena will now be my second in command.'

Everyone cheered and the automatic doors opened again and in walked, Roella and Shalaine who had come to join them. Everyone was in high spirits and mingled together as friends would do. Some were a little awed by Barooks presence, but he showed them that he had a friendly side as well as a firm leader's side too.

Chapter Seventeen

Getting back to normal:

Barook was back on Annarki, his home planet, and was speaking with his councillors about the escape of Sholok, 'I am going to send out six ships to the nearest star systems that Sholock might have gone to, we can't afford to let him find another race of aliens and create another army and come back to attack us. We now have the Tachyon drive engines fitted to our space ships and can get to the nearest star systems before, Sholock. We may even catch him up or even overtake him. That would be the hope and to bring him back here for trial.'

His six councillors with him were, Coolan, Melchio, Flane, Shikon, Killoon and Tranio. They were the main ones who helped make the final decisions with Barook. Tranio looked at Barook, 'Do you think we will be able to find them, Barook, he could be anywhere, even on a moon somewhere we don't know about?' he asked.

'I know that possibility exists, Tranio, but if we don't find him, we have the risk of him rising again, and we haven't explored the nearer star systems because we haven't had the power of the Tachyon drive engines. They will allow us to travel faster than the speed of light and catch him up. His spacecraft is not anywhere as fast as ours are, we could feasibly overtake him and capture him and his crew, which would be my preference. I don't want to destroy his craft and those with him. I promised Lurack that I would try my best to bring his father back to him, and I will honour that if it is at all possible.'

Coolan then asked, 'What will you do with Sholok if we catch him and get him back alive?'

'I think we all know the answer to that question, Coolan, he will go to the Prison moon and I don't think he will last very long there, the Greylon bodies are not built for the kind of work they are expected to do. The other Greylon's that have gone there in the past have only lasted a few weeks, and I expect that to be the case with Sholok. My point is, I shall have kept my side of the bargain with Lurack, and I'll give his father and the other crew members a chance to become faithful members of the society and live in peace with everyone else, I have a feeling that none of them really wanted to go with Sholok.'

Coolan nodded to him, 'Yes, Barook, I know what you are saying, but Skolok is treacherous enough to kill them all and won't surrender.

'Your point is noted, Coolan, but I think Sholok wants to live as much as anyone else, I doubt he'll kill himself and the others, unless he is completely mad.'

They all laughed at Barook's comment, Shikon one of the other councillors asked, 'Barook, What is going to become of the Greylon's planet, much of its resources are mined out, that is why they wanted to takeover Thaldernian?'

'We will have wait and see on that point, Shikon, let's get Sholok caught first and his crew sorted, then we'll consider that, however, there are several moons in our system that can be mined, we can let them mine what they wish from those if need be,'

'That is true, Barook, I think that would solve their problem, let's hope we catch Sholok, I think everybody will feel safer then.'

Barook agreed and they continued to discuss the affairs that needed sorting immediately.

More machinery had been brought by the Annarkians to the new city site and the foundations had been completed. All was ready now for the Cornerstone Ceremony that the Annarkians did when a new city was about to be started. They were now excavating large stones and rock to form the base layer of the buildings This was been quarried from various parts of the land that was some distance away from the site, but was being brought by large transporter craft and laid ready for placing in the foundations. They would move them into place with antigravity devices that made sure each rock was in the exact right place.

Barook was planning to come the day after to perform the ceremony, from then on, the city would be started and the first buildings would be erected. There was to be a mixed workforce of Annarkians and Neanderthals, everyone contributing with their different skills. Many of the Neanderthals were to be trained to used some of the very technological machinery so they could be more useful, but not used as slaves as the rebels tried to suggest. The Neanderthals were well paid and in line with the Annarkians.

Norak, together with Scaroon were to be overseers when the site got started and would be part of the council to run the city when completed.

Scaroon came in the door of Francesca's apartment and went to Francesca who was in the kitchen section preparing their evening meal, 'Hello my lover, what kind of day have you had today?' he asked as he walked up behind her and hugged from her rear.

She turned and smiled at him and gave him a long lingering kiss, 'I've had a good day at the shop, it seems that now there is no rebel threats, people are showing more interest in the weapons,' Francesca told him.

'I can believe that, I think before, they were frightened of being linked with the rebels and didn't want to be seen with the guns and bows etc. The Gun Club is growing in membership too, probably for the same reasons and are no longer in fear of being accused of being a rebel,' he said.

'That is good, Scaroon, I'm pleased for everyone, we can now live in peace. We even had an Annarki man come into the shop today, he was interested in the crossbows and long bows, he said they were all intrigued by the ancient weapons and that more were wanting to learn how to use them, they may even come and join your club, Scaroon,' Francesca said with a wide smile.'

Scaroon laughed at her words, 'Well, Francesca, we have plenty of room, I am making plans to extend the rear of the archery gallery so more people can practice. The bows and crossbows are becoming more popular than the guns,' he said.

Scaroon noticed there was an extra place laid at the table, 'Are we having someone visit for tea?' he asked her.

'Yes, Norak is coming to chat with us about the city, the foundations are finished and Barook is holding a cornerstone ceremony tomorrow around mid day to officially give the start to the building work.'

'That sounds interesting.'

Scaroon had just got the words out as a knock came to the door. He went over and opened it to greet Norak.

'Good evening, Norak, come in and join us, we are it seems expecting you. Francesca says it's to do with the new city.'

'Yes, Scaroon, Barook is coming from Annarki tomorrow and should be here about mid day; apparently they always have a cornerstone ceremony when starting

189

to build a new city. We are invited to be amongst the VIP guests.'

'Sounds good, please sit down at the table, Norak, dinner is about ready.'

Norak sniffed at the aroma floating from the kitchen, 'Mm, that smells delicious, Francesca, what are you cooking?' he asked.

'I'm cooking a chicken dish cooked in stock with white wine added, it was a favourite dish my mother used to do and was always very welcomed by the family.'

'I can't wait, I'm very hungry. The town had been very busy today, I think more people are moving here to work on the city site, quite a number of our people have been given jobs there,' Norak said.

Moments later, Francesca put a full plate of wine flavoured chicken in front of the two men complete with potatoes and various vegetables. She then brought hers and joined them.

When they had finished eating, Norak said, 'That was absolutely delicious, Francesca, your mother taught you well.'

'Thank you, Norak. So what have you to tell us?'

'Well, firstly, Voix has been shipped to the Prison Moon and is now out of the way, but the main thing is that the city is going to have many new things and our children are going to have a daily educational program with two days off at the end of the week. They are going to learn many subjects and brought up to date with the Annarki technology and histories. I think we shall begin to see what the Annarki can really do. The children will grow up to be very up to date with everything that's on offer and we shall progress very quickly as the years pass.'

'That's wonderful, Norak,' Francesca said, 'if only the rebels had have trusted them more, there wouldn't have been no trouble of any kind.'

Scaroon went quiet at hearing the words from Francesca, 'I feel very bad about my involvement with the rebels, I should have waited until things happened and have seen for myself what the Annarki really had in store for our people.'

Norak felt the sadness in Scaroons voice, 'Scaroon, you shouldn't feel bad, your decision to help us saved many from being killed, if the rebels had have attacked the Annarki and even those of our people who were not rebels, many would have died or been badly injured. Barook knows it was hard for you to betray Voix, but he was a bad man and no one saw it coming, no one suspected him to be the high council traitor, I worked with him and he'd fooled me,' Norak said to him.

Francesca knew how Scaroon felt and had talked to her about his feelings, 'Scaroon, what Norak says is true, you have been given a new start and your Gun Club is going well, be happy that you were brave enough to expose Voix, that took a lot of courage,' she told him.

Scaroon just looked up at them both and said, 'I did what I came here to do, that was my priority. When I learned that Voix was the cause of my brother's death, it was the logical thing to do, to expose him instead of killing him, which I seriously considered.'

'You did the right thing, Scaroon and everyone is grateful to you for your actions, Barook is particularly pleased with you,' Norak said.

'I guess we shall have to see what happens from now on, it can only get better and soon Francesca and I can be officially mated.' Scaroon added.

'That will be a day to look forward to Scaroon,' Norak said.

Barook was standing with his six spaceship captains who were going to search for Sholok. He was hoping they would find him and bring him back alive. 'Listen all of you, I want you to try and bring back Sholok alive with all his crew. Remember what I have promised Lurak, I want to see him reunited with his father who is one of the crew that went with Sholok, Travel well and search the six systems we have that are closest to ours, I'm sure you will find him at one of them somewhere.'

Ashtuk was going with them in his ship too, 'Barook, what shall we do when we find him, do we trap him in space or take him to the nearest planet, considering he could be anywhere?' he asked.

Barook looked at Ashtuk and then to the other captains, 'When you find him, you contact me immediately by the trans-space communications. I will have a ship ready and waiting and will come to who has found him. Also, the ship that finds him will need to contact the other five ships so they can come to the one who has found Sholok. Whatever you do, do not contact him until I get to you, just keep him under surveillance.'

All the captains nodded and understood Barook's orders and would follow them to the letter. They turned and left Barook and headed for their spacecraft.

It didn't take long before each search craft was lifting up to go in search of Sholok. Barook watched them as each ship disappeared above the clouds and went into space. He truly hoped they would find Sholok and his crew.

Barook didn't see the young man who was standing a short distance away from him, it was Lurak. He turned and saw the lad watching him, 'Hello, Lurak. I take it you saw the captains go off in their ships. They have gone to find Sholok and hopefully his crew. I truly hope they find them without any deaths, I will look forward and hope we shall see your father again, but please be patient, space is vast and they will take time to search for them. I will inform you when I know something,' he assured Lurak.

Lurack walked up to him, 'Lord Barook, when you go to the ships when they find Sholok, may I come with you?'

Barook smiled at him, 'Well, Lurak, in all fairness, I think considering the potential dangers, I would feel better if you stayed here. Now you have come to Annarki, you have plenty to occupy yourself with and much to learn, please be patient,' Barook said hoping he would understand.

'I know what you are saying, Lord Barook, I will respect your request for me to stay here, but I hope that my father is found safe and that Sholok will get his just deserves.'

Barook smiled at him and said, 'Fear not, Lurak, if we get Sholok back alive, he will be getting his justice and be joining the other rebels on the prison moon.'

'Thank you, Lord Barook, the sooner that happens the better I will feel.'

'Yes, Lurak, so will everyone else. Come, let us go and eat together and discuss your future, I think you have a lot to look forward to.'

Lurak walked with Barook and headed to a nearby eating-place and both enjoyed a good meal and drink and discussed many things that Lurak could do in the near future. Barook had plans for him and had taken a strong liking to the lad and wanted to see him do well.

Everyone was gathered to the meeting place for the Cornerstone Ceremony. Barook had brought young Lurak with him too to enjoy the event. Barook looked round at everyone and realised that just about every member of the local town and many others had come to see the placing of the cornerstone.

'Good day to everyone of you, I didn't expect this amount of people, but I'm pleased to see you have come to get things off to a good start. I would like to say before manoeuvring the first stone in place, that this is the start of not only the building of this new city, but a start of a new era for us all. This city will contain many facilities for everyone to use and learn from. We have already organised teachers for the children's classes and instructors for teaching the men and women who are going to be helping build this city. We shall go on to build other cities around your planet and expand the populations in a big way. I will now press the button that will lower this large cornerstone into place.' Barook pushed the bright transparent crystal button on the anti-gravity sledge and the rock moved into place and came to its rest. Everyone cheered and looked forward to see the city begin to grow.

Chapter Eighteen

In Search of Sholok:

After the Cornerstone Ceremony, Barook and Norak went back to Norak's Pavilion to discuss immediate plans for the future of the city and for Barook to tell Norak about Sholok and what he intended to do. Norak knew that the Greylon planet had been taken over by the Annarki, but didn't know much about Sholok and those who escaped with him.

'Barook, what are your plans concerning Sholok, if he has escaped into space, he could be anywhere. It will be a mammoth task trying to find him?' Norak asked.

'Well, we now have more powerful weapons and also a new advanced drive system for our ships that will travel several times faster than the speed of light, you do understand what I mean by the speed of light, don't you, Norak?' Barook asked him.

'Yes, Barook, I understand this, even though we don't have a flying craft technology, I do know the concept of light speed.'

'That's good, as we can now outrun any spacecraft known to us, meaning, we can catch up with Sholok's craft. There are six star systems within our reach that are only a few light-years from us, I have sent out six ships to search for Skolok and fully anticipate our ships overtaking his ship before it reaches another planet to establish a settlement on. His ship is not equipped with such engines like ours and he will take a very long time to reach the nearest star system, which is the, Doonar system. I have sent my best captain towards this system as I think that Sholok will head for the nearest of them.'

'Are you sure he has gone towards another star system, there are several planets and moons in our own that he could escape to and reach them quite quickly?'

'If he did that, Norak, we would pick his ship up on our radar scanners. We have them all under surveillance and some we are probing with view to use for different reasons.'

'I see, well I wish you the best of luck in finding him, he certainly needs to be caught and sent to your prison moon.'

'I can assure you, Norak, we will find him, no matter how long it takes. We have the technology to do it now and ships to travel fast enough to catch him. I'm expecting to hear from the scout ships very soon.'

'That's good, Barook, but to change the subject, I think that our people are looking forward to starting their new jobs in the new site tomorrow. Now they know you are not going to make slaves of them, as the rebels tried to convince them of, the city should progress very quickly. I for one look forward to seeing it finished and everything in place.

'Yes, Norak, so do I, it is one of many we plan to build. We know there are other Neanderthal settlements on your planet and we intend to help all of them one by one. We want Thaldernian to be our second world and home so we can make it like ours, we are very benevolent people and want to see your people advance and one day become a technological race like ours.'

'That will be good, Barook, we as an individual race are many generations off developing your technology, maybe thousands of years. We will look forward to your advanced teachings.'

Barook and Norak chatted at length about the new city and the advancement of the Neanderthals. At the end of the day, Barook took his leave of Norak and headed back to his own planet to see how things were progressing and hoped he would hear from the scout ships out looking for Sholok very soon.

Barook was in his personal quarters reading some recent reports from his councillors when one of his men came to him very excited, 'My Lord Barook, Ashtuk is waiting to speak with you, he is on the monitor waiting to speak.'

'Very well, Borid, switch him through and I'll take his transmission on my monitor in this room.' Barook stood up and turned on his personal monitor that he could speak to anyone and anywhere on the planet or outer space. Moments later, Ashtuk appeared on the screen.

Barook was keen to hear what he had to say, 'I hope you have good news for me, Ashtuk, have you found Sholok?'

Ashtuk smiled at him, 'I think so, My Lord Barook, we have picked up a ship on our distant viewer monitor what could be his ship. We are gaining on him very fast and expect to be within range very shortly.'

That is good, Ashtuk, I will keep this monitor open for your transmission for when you reach him. I will not need to come to you, I am able to conduct the necessary work from here and deal with Sholok.'

'Very well, My Lord, I will come back to you as soon as we make contact.' The monitor in Barook's room went off and Barook was feeling very pleased with Ashtuk's news and hoped it was Sholok's ship, then realised that it was the only ship it could be, they had never encountered any other aliens other than the Greylons.

It was only a short time later when Barook's monitor sprung back into operation and Ashtuk was there ready to speak with him, 'My Lord Barook, we have them in contact distance, I am about to try and make contact, do you wish to remain on line whilst we do so?' Ashtuk asked him.

'Yes, Ashtuk, do it now, I want to see if Sholok shows himself.'

'Very well, My Lord.' Ashtuk spoke into the monitor to contact Sholok, 'This is Ashtuk calling,

Sholok, answer this request and speak with us or we will destroy you.'

Barook knew that Ashtuk was only saying this to frighten Sholok into speaking with him. Moments later, Sholok showed himself on the monitor, 'How in hell did you catch us up, our spacecraft are faster than yours, or at least they were?' Sholok asked him sounding very angry.'

Ashtuk looked at Sholok straight in the eyes and answered, 'We now have tachyon drive engines that can help us travel several times faster than light. It was your scientists who joined us that brought the technology with them. They had had enough of your tyrannical rule and came to us with their ideas. We also have more powerful weapons than you, so don't try firing at us, it would be futile.'

Sholok knew he had been caught and wasn't going to get away. 'He looked at Ashtuk and answered, 'I will make you a bargain, I will let you have my crew, but I stay aboard my ship. I can operate it automatically by myself.'

Ashtuk looked at him and answered, 'I will give it some thought, Sholok and get back to you very soon.' Ashtuk delayed Sholok's transmission for a moment whilst he spoke to Barook. He turned to the monitor that Barook was waiting on, 'My Lord, did you hear what Sholok asked, he wants to stay on his ship, but will allow his crew to leave and come to us.'

Barook looked at Ashtuk, 'So he wants to bargain with us does he, well, we will let him send his crew to us first and then I'll think about what we'll do next. Tell him you agree to his terms and let him send his crew to you so we know they are safe.'

'Very well, My Lord Barook, I will do that.' Ashtuk contacted Sholok again and he came back on the screen. 'Sholok, I have considered your request and accept it, send all your crew to my ship immediately and then you can do as you will, but do it now,' he told Sholok.

Sholok gave instruction for his crew to go to Ashtuk's ship on their shuttle. All the crew of Sholok's craft did as Sholok told them and set off to Ashtuk's ship. It didn't take them long before they reached Ashtuks craft and were met by guards and were told that any tricks and they would be exterminated. None of them tried anything and were happy to be out of Sholok's way. None of them wanted to be with him as they knew their lives would be of no worth working with Sholok, but were surprised that Ashtuk agreed with Sholok to let him stay on his own ship alone.

All Sholok's men were temporally put into a secure holding bay until it was decided what was to happen to them. Ashtuk looked at Barook again who was waiting to hear what was happening.

'My Lord Barook, we now have the men from Sholok's ship aboard ours and have them in the secure holding bay. What are your instructions for Sholok?'

'Contact Sholok and tell him that you want him alive and to surrender himself or you will destroy his ship.'

'Very well, My Lord,' Ashtuk looked at the monitor he'd spoken to Sholok on and transmitted to him to contact him again. Moments later, Sholok came onto the monitor, 'What is it, Ashtuk, you have my men, now I get to go my way.'

'I'm afraid that Lord Barook has told me that you have to surrender or die, the choice is yours, Sholok, you have two minutes to decide,' Ashtuk told him.

'You have tricked me, I will destroy your ship,' Sholok said and suddenly Ashtuk saw flashes of light coming from Sholok's ship as he began to fire on his.

Ashtuk gave the command to destroy Sholok's weapons as they came closer with their new beam weapon. Each of the weapons were blasted before getting anywhere near to Ashtuk's ship. Ashtuk then heard Barook say, 'Destroy his ship and put an end to him, he wouldn't last long on the prison moon anyway.'

'Yes, My Lord,' Astuk said and gave the command for the weapon to be fired at Sholok's ship. Within seconds, Sholok's ship was vaporised by the new beam weapons and was no more, only a void of space remained where Sholok's ship had been.

Ashtuk looked at the monitor that Barook was looking from, 'My Lord, Sholok is no more, we have destroyed him and his ship.'

Barook looked at Ashtuk with a contented expression and nodded, 'Very well, Ashtuk, now I wish you to make sure that the man called Curin is amongst the crew of Sholok's men and have him brought to the control room so I can see him. Contact me when you have him with you.'

'Very well, My Lord, I will send for him immediately,' Ashtuk said and Barook disappeared from the monitor and waited until Curin was brought to the control room of Ashtuk's ship.

It wasn't long before Curin had been brought to the control room where he now stood with Ashtuk waiting for Barook to come on screen. He was curious why Barook would want to talk to him. Moments later, Barook appeared on the monitor and looked at Ashtuk and the man standing with him.

'Am I to take it that your name is Curin, the father of Lurack?' he asked him.

Curin looked at him with concern and wondered if anything had happened to his son, 'Yes, My Lord, Barook, I am the Father of Lurack, is my son all right?' he asked.

Barook laughed at him for a few moments, 'Oh yes, Curin, he is very well, but a very high spirited young man, he dared to take a pop-shot at me when I went to Greylon, but as you can see, I'm still alive.'

Curin was shocked, 'Oh no, is he apprehended? I will be having words with him about that when I see him, I offer my humblest apologies, My Lord Barook for my son's actions.'

'I did that for you, Curin and had some very stern words with him, but we came to an agreement, he promised me he would work for me if I brought you back alive. I am aware that none of the crew on Sholok's ship wanted to go with him, that is why I wanted you all back alive, Sholok is now dead and gone. He tried to fire on us, but we destroyed him and his ship, he'll bother no one again.'

'Then I am in your debt, My Lord, I too pledge my alliance with you, and I'm sure our other men will too, but we had to follow orders or be killed by Sholok.'

'I know this, Curin. You and your men will be brought back and reunited with their families. The Greylon people are already settling into a better way of life than what they had before. I think they will be happier under Annarki rule.'

Ashtuk smiled at Barook, 'I will now show the Greylon's to better quarters until we get back to Annarki, we will set off immediately.'

'Very well, Ashtuk, we will see you soon.'

Barook had now kept his side of the bargain with Lurack and looked forward to reuniting him with his father, it was to be arranged as soon as Ashtuk got back their own planet.

The trip back was very good and all the other ships were recalled back to Annarki too, they hadn't found anything else and were glad to be coming back home.

Lurack was sitting in his room reading when Barook came into it through the automatic door. Barook had been told Lurack's door code and wanted to surprise him. 'Hello, Lurack, how are you today?' he asked the lad.

'I'm well thank you, My Lord. To what do I owe this visit from this planet's leader, I feel honoured?'

'There is someone I want you to meet, Lurack, he has been looking forward to seeing you.'

Lurack wasn't sure what Barook meant and asked, 'Who would want to meet me, I am just a lowly Greylon?'

At that moment, Curin walked in and opened his arms to greet his son, 'Hello, Lurack, how are you my Son, I hear you've taken up making pop-shots at the Annarki leader, not a good idea, Son.'

Lurack jumped to his feet and went to greet his father with a big hug. 'Father, it's so good to see you again, I'm so glad you are alive, Lord Barook promised me he would bring you back, but I have to say that I was

worried,' Lurack turned to Barook and said two words,
'**Thank you.**'

The End

Printed in Great Britain
by Amazon